Mary A. Denison

That Wife of Mine

Mary A. Denison

That Wife of Mine

ISBN/EAN: 9783744790208

Printed in Europe, USA, Canada, Australia, Japan

Cover: Foto ©Andreas Hilbeck / pixelio.de

More available books at **www.hansebooks.com**

THAT WIFE OF MINE.

BY THE AUTHOR OF

"THAT HUSBAND OF MINE."

————◆————

BOSTON:

LEE AND SHEPARD, PUBLISHERS.

NEW YORK:

CHARLES T. DILLINGHAM.

1877.

In the "Editor's Drawer" of HARPER'S MAGAZINE, a few years ago, the question was asked, "Why will not some one of our American writers give us a series of domestic sketches, — actual occurrences of every-day life, — the exact truthfulness and aptness of which will at once touch a chord that will instantly vibrate in the popular heart, — the real joys and sorrows of the home circle?"

"THAT HUSBAND OF MINE," and its companion volume, "THAT WIFE OF MINE," by the same author, are designed to answer this question.

Electrotyped and Printed by
Rand, Avery, and Company,
117 Franklin Street,
Boston.

DEDICATED

TO

THE SAME PARTIES

AS

"THAT HUSBAND OF MINE,"

BY

THE SAME AUTHOR.

THAT WIFE OF MINE.

Chapter One.

I DECLARE to the tocsin!"

"Charlie!" exclaimed my little wife breathlessly, springing to her feet.

"Lissa," said I with equal vehemence, "it must be that the emperor of all the Russias is dead, and I am summoned to write his obituary in the '·Regulator.'"

"I should think somebody was dead — such a peal as that!" and my wife thrust her sewing into her work-basket, and turned to the door as it opened.

"Why, what is the matter of it, Jo? What is it?" and Lissa, subsiding into her pretty broken language, as she always did when startled or nervous, addressed herself to a face that at that moment looked in.

"A baby," said Jo, in an awful voice.

"A what?" cried I, rising up in consternation, as my sister by degrees introduced her whole body, and stood with speculative face inside the door.

"Why, somebody has left one on the doorstep, — a sweet and helpless infant," continued Jo, shaking the one pensive ringlet in the middle of her forehead.

"Oh, dear me!" said Lissa, turning to me, "is it not strange? *I* don't want it: do you, Charlie?"

"Of course not, my dear," was my answer. "I've no special predilection for any thing that don't belong to me. What is it, Jo? Where was it left? and what have you done with it? Was that the reason of the violent ring that just now sounded through the house?"

"Yes, brother Charlie: Tiddy was busy setting the table for tea, and I was taking out the preserves, when we heard the bell. Tiddy went to the door. 'Vow to *my* rest!' cried Tiddy. 'Come here, Miss Jo. Ef that ain't an affliction of Providence!' Then I saw the baby. It was fast asleep, a pretty little thing."

"I'll send it to the poorhouse forthwith!" I exclaimed. "Somebody has been playing an infamous trick on me."

Lissa, my little wife, crept closer and closer. She now stood with her slight fingers upon my arm, looking into my eyes.

"Charlie," she whispered, "I have been thinking. Don't send it away. That's just how I was left," she added softly.

"What, at some man's door?"

"No, no, but alone — all alone — fatherless, motherless; who to take care of me but one poor lad? Oh! I feel a pity for the little one; for I was so young, so helpless, when my mother died."

And I pause here to let the reader know something of this little wife of mine.

Sweet Elsa had gone from me. I had mourned her for three long years.

At first, after I laid her head on its cold pillow, I felt that life was no longer endurable. The home so bright held still the charm of her presence; but it was nothing that I could clasp in my arms, and kiss; it was nothing that I could sit beside, and feel the glance of gentle eyes upon me, as I read during the long winter evenings: it only threw a chill over my very soul from its lack of love and life. Consequently I gave up my home. I went abroad as special correspondent of "The Regulator" and other papers. I travelled all over England and Wales on foot. I went to Germany, and was pursuing the same course there.

One day, in an odd little straggling town in the south of Germany, I met with an accident. My horse did not throw me in some picturesque spot with my head on a pile of rocks, for somebody to find after a romantic fashion ; for I had no horse. Neither did chaise or diligence or coach break down. I simply jumped carelessly, and hurt my foot.

It was in one of the long gray twilights of that part of the world ; and a pale moon had just come out white and clearly defined, throwing the rugged hills, the stony country, the uneven streets, into bright and homely outline. After trying to walk for a few seconds, I found that the jump had rendered my foot quite useless ; and I had taken my seat by the roadside, and was proceeding to pull off my shoe, when a tall, handsome-looking student as I thought, came out of a low doorway, and over the loose stones, to me.

"I can't talk German," I said, a little impatiently; "and I believe I have really hurt myself."

"Ah, you are English! so I can talk with *you*, you see," were the words that saluted my ears. I don't know that I ever felt a sensation so closely resembling rapture, as I did at the sound of mine own familiar tongue.

"I have done myself some injury, I don't know what," I said, after a glad, long shake of the hand.

"Then you shall come over to my house," he responded. "Can you walk if I help you, or shall my sister come to give aid also?"

I managed with his arm to get to the house. It was a curious little home, the lower flat all one room, with a shining brown floor. Just outside the window I saw a kind of open kitchen, in which a brisk old woman whose face was the color of parchment, under a glorious wealth of silver-white hair, moved about round the fire, preparing the evening meal. Beyond that was the garden, just glooming in spots, but still bright and rich with color, full of fruit-trees from which pears and apples hung, the trellises and the walls loaded with vines whose clusters of grapes looked to me

something marvellous.   It was a quaintly and
beautifully colored picture ; for still farther beyond
were rocks from which stood out bold ledges like
ruined and forsaken castles, and these caught the
wonderful color of the far setting sun, and threw
the warm tones like drifts of sparkling nebulæ
back upon the garden.

"Lissa!" called the man, after he had settled
me to my liking ; and then I saw a flitting figure
far down the long old yard, that stood for a
moment in strong contrast with the whitewashed
trellis.   It was clad in a red petticoat, white, loose,
large-sleeved blouse, and had a pretty cap perched
upon its head.   The skirt was short, showing
beautifully moulded ankles ; and the feet, which
I was sure were small and pretty, were incased in
wooden shoes.

"Yes, Conrad," answered back the voice ; and a
soft, low, musical tone it was, such as I had never
heard since Elsa left me.   Then she came quietly
along the middle and flagged path, her queer shoes
clicking at every step.

Heavens and earth ! what was there about the
child-woman that brought my Elsa before me ?
She was a little creature ; and for Elsa's sake I

love these dainty, tiny women, the fern-leaf and blossom of humanity. •I could have taken her straightway to my heart, as if she had been of kin to me, and kissed her on the forehead over which hung light rings of glossy golden-brown hair, almost in the exact fashion my darling had worn them when I first knew her. Curiously I wondered if she was like Elsa in other respects, — the sunny temper, the sweet, forgiving disposition, the quick, clear intuition, almost like a gospel to both of us. Conrad spoke a few words in German, which I understood; and the girl turned her face toward me, a little clouded with pity, and immediately ran out in the kitchen, soon re-appearing with a basin of warm water and a soft sponge, carrying also a long, large-necked bottle of some dark solution. Then the gray servant came in, and bathed my foot while I reclined on an old yellow settee; and Lissa, from whom I could hardly, keep my eyes, lifted a square slab from the side of the wall, covered it with a snowy cloth, and presently the table was set, the board spread with fruit, a black loaf, pats of yellow butter, milk, cheese, and tea. They drew the settee up with me on it, and I supped deliciously.

Then I learned that Conrad was a teacher, called there professor ; that he was in reality an exceptional genius, deeply read in the sciences, a traveller who had made much of his experience ; and that with all this he had taken the sole care of his sister from the time she was a year old, saving that at certain periods Mrs. Gretchen, the old family servant, had superintended her domestic education.

After a delightful evening, I found that with some help I could get up stairs, where Conrad gave me his own room. He himself **slept** out in the quaintly carved balcony, which he said he often did of warm nights. Glorious days succeeded, in that pleasant German household. I was placed in Lissa's care ; and she and I had long and cheerful talks, for she knew English imperfectly, but so that I could understand her, while I failed to make my German translatable. I told her much of my past, of my Elsa; indeed, she always brought the conversation round to Elsa, and there were so many points in which I traced resemblances, that **it is** not wonderful if I felt in a vague way, that **the** sweet woman's loss was almost made up to me.

From **her I learned such** facts as gave me that

exalted estimation in which I have always since held the professor Conrad von Raab.

"Do you know," she said (I will not give her broken English, which would not be music to your ear as it was to mine), "I have never known any protector, any father, any mother, save in my brother Conrad. When I was left a little babe of only one year, he would give me up to nobody. He was only eighteen then, and just through with his studies at the university ; but he took all the care of me when he was at home. And when I was quite grown, about nine, and he had become famous for his genius, and an old uncle left him some money, oh ! it seemed a great fortune. Then he took me with him wherever he went, and would let nobody watch me or teach me but himself. We left good old Gretchen in this little house, which belongs to Conrad, and we travelled, oh, all over the world ; and Conrad made friends in the universities, and studied hard, and wrote lectures ; and I helped him," she added, her beautiful face aglow.

"And how did you help him ? " I asked.

"I carried his hammer and his bag, and labelled his specimens, and found subjects for his micro-

scope, — you should see his microscopes, — and I
copied his lectures sometimes ; for, do you know,
he says I write a beautiful clear hand.   And everywhere we went, people made much of us, so that at
last it seemed strange to come home here, and settle down.   But we are going to move again, and
where do you think ? "

" To some other town ? " I ventured.

" Oh, no ! " and she clapped her hands glee-
fully, — " to America ! to your own country, — to
the land where you were so happy with your Elsa,
and where you left her, as you said, with your poor
heart all crushed."

I told her then, almost in a whisper, that she
looked like Elsa, that her voice and her ways made
me think of her ; and the innocent child listened
with cheeks aglow, and eyes shining, and — and
then followed a beautiful idyllic season ; and it
came to pass, after a few months' sojourn, that I
held a second Elsa close to my breast, and kissed
her forehead, her cheeks, and her lips, for she
loved me, and Conrad gave his glad consent.   So
we were all to go to America together.

And that is how I won my precious wife, — my
careless, positive, whimsical, loving wife, endowed

with a thousand freaks, humors, and oddities, but charming in every one of them, and who makes me exclaim, sometimes with frantic vehemence, sometimes with frowns, sometimes with laugh-ter, —

"Oh, that wife of mine!"

Chapter Two.

E were married in the little German house, the birthplace of my bride, and set off directly for America. Lissa took a comical leave of all the surroundings, — the old settee in the balcony, in which Conrad had rocked her to sleep so many times; the precious relics of her dead mother, which she could not carry with her; the garden, sunny with the memories of her seventeen bright years. The tears were in her eyes, and in mine too; and when the carriage came, and we missed her all suddenly, and there was not a minute to lose, everybody was seized with consternation.

"Lissa!" cried Conrad. "Lissa!" echoed in every corner and cranny of the house. Up flew one to the garret, out flew another to the garden. It was my good luck to find her at last, weeping over some pet kittens in a room above the barn,

where also was stored a collection such as my eyes
never gazed upon before, — the playthings of a
motherless child. These were made up mainly of
broken material, cast-off relics, torn books, muti-
lated plaster images, a stuffed dog in the last
stages of laceration, a swing, and two eyeless
dolls, which must have owed their existence to the
awkward hands of some neophyte in wood-carving,
and, as I learned afterwards, the work of the inde-
fatigable Conrad.

"Lissa," I said, "the carriage waits."

"Send it away," she said imperatively: "I can't
go."

I stood petrified for a moment, not knowing what
to say.

"Do you think I am going to leave every thing
for ever and ever, every thing that I love, for you?"
and the accumulated force of her over-wrought
feelings made her smooth voice sound like the
voice of a scold, peevish and shrill, as she sobbed.

Aghast, I still kept silence.

"Why don't you speak? Don't you see I re-
pent at the last minute? I'm not a bit like Elsa:
you needn't tell me that, I see it in your face.
Where are you going?"

"To order the carriage back," I said gently.

She sprang up, and made a passionate gesture with her hands across her eyes.

"There! that's the last of Lissa Von Raab. Don't you know you never should mind when I ask such unreasonable things — you, a great, strong man? Conrad has spoiled me, but I am only his sister: I am your wife, and I said I would obey you."

She held out her hands, forming as pretty a picture of angelic womanhood as I ever saw, and of course you know how it ended. There was a little smothered sigh, and a little smothered kiss; and, after she had dried her eyes on my shoulder, she went with me as gentle as any lamb, never once looking behind at the uncouth treasure-house, at which I could have laughed till I cried but for the solemn tenderness her love wrought within me, and that made these monstrosities sacred in my sight.

Conrad was a prize. He contracted friendships on board the steamer, that proved worth a fine income when he reached what he always called the garden of the world. I made up my mind, to Lissa's delight, that we two could not part with him ; and, on our arrival, events had so shaped themselves as to make still more feasible his adoption into our family. My aunt Jack was dead, and had left me a handsome sum in her will; and, the senior editor of "The Regulator" having resigned, I was offered the post, with a large increase of salary. I was now comparatively a rich man. Lissa was installed in a new and elegant home, with my half-sister Joanna, who, since my mother's death, had been the special charge of aunt Jack, and who was left to me along with the money.

I was very glad to welcome Jo. She was only a few years my junior, of a youthful, romantic temperament; but, as time disclosed, a little inclined to tyrannize, and to consider her way in every point the only right way. Old Tiddy, who had also gone West with my aunt, and who, during the life of my parents, had been a fixture as a family servant, also reverted back to me; and, with these additions, my household was complete.

So there you have us all at the period when that blessed baby was left at our door, and Lissa, contrary to my expectations, pleaded that I would not take it to the poorhouse.

But, before I go on with this peculiar domestic episode, I must present to you, in order tó make the thread of my story more even, my wife's brother, —

The professor.

Chapter Three.

AKE my baby, sir, only a minute! I'll be back soon."

A staid professor, with blue spectacles, wandering aimlessly about with a baby in his arms! Who put it there he could not tell, only that a wild-looking woman rushed into the little depot, and quite thrust it upon him, then disappeared.

What should he do with it?

It was lying very quietly now, — a fair little bundle of white wraps, and a still, innocent face.

The professor looked east and looked west,— nothing but woods, woods, as far as could be seen, and between the weeds the glimmer of two iron rails. Away off in the distance a young woman was walking, in a red calico dress and a green sunbonnet. She came nearer and nearer. The professor trembled to see her coming; and he could hardly have told why, except that he was alone with the baby.

The young woman looked in, rustic fashion, then spoke out, —

" La ! how pretty it is ! "

The young man blushed to his forehead, and pulled his wide-brimmed hat closer over his eyes. The young man, I said : well, he was but thirty-five, and hardly looked thirty. A tall, rather spare edition of the *genus homo;* a man with a scientific cast of nose, and great tender, beautiful, dreamy eyes, that it seemed a shame to disguise with blue eye-glasses.

But then, the professor was near-sighted, very near-sighted. It was a positive terror to him to go without glasses. He was always running into people. Therefore he kept seven pairs in different places, to meet the demands which a sometimes forgetful habit imposed upon him, — one in each of his waistcoat-pockets, one pair always hanging in sight in his room, and three others locked carefully away. These would all change places in due course of time, but it rarely happened that he lost track of them all at once.

And now what should he do with the baby ?

The young woman in the red gown was fast disappearing : she was gone. Almost any common man would have laid it down, and let it take its chance of being found; but our professor was not a common man. He vaguely kept hoping that the wild, anxious, rather handsome young person who had so unceremoniously invested him with this strange charge would make her appearance again. He wandered to and fro. How still it was, save the monotonous breathing of the forest harmony, and the shrill chirping of many insects! He walked this side and that, wondering, if he should be recognized as the lecturer of the previous evening, what people would say of his dubious position as a *pro-tem.* family man.

The baby still slept. On its little face was impressed an angelic sweetness that touched his heart, but nevertheless he longed to be rid of the baby. His brain was in a mist: it always was in a mist about ordinary things. He knew possibly, theoretically, that mutton was sheep; but whether it was cut up to boil, or boiled whole and then dissected, I think he would have been unable to tell. But talk to him of the systems of stars, ecliptical signs, or the Greek constellations, and he was perfectly at home, and would charm and dazzle by the hour with his brilliant theories and delightful speculations.

But the baby! Time was passing on leaden wings, and still nobody came.

Except a hand-car full of roughs, which stopped barely long enough to let out old Perkins, the man who had charge of the lamps. He nodded to the professor.

"A fine boy that, gineral," he said.

"I wonder if it *is* a boy," thought the professor.

"Usually travel with your family, gineral?" was the next remark, with a twinkle of the cunning old eyes hid away behind the wrinkles.

"Yes, always — I beg your pardon — no; I haven't any family," blundered the professor, who jocosely called a certain apparatus with which he sometimes illustrated his lectures, his family.

"Oh!" and the old fellow gave him a searching, sidelong look from under his beetling brows.

"This is not my child. I walked down from Morristown this morning : I have been botanizing, and collecting stones for specimens, till within an hour or so. While I was alone here, a woman ran in, and threw the child in my arms. What am I to do with it?"

The old man chuckled.

"*I* don't want it, any how; and, as to the woman, why maybe she'll be at the keers when they come. I don't git here but onct a day. Ain't you the man that lectered up to Morristown last night? You lect'rers are a poplar sort of people, you are," and he chuckled again.

The poor professor felt his courage oozing out in large drops at the thought of being recognized. He tried to disengage one hand in order to get at his handkerchief; but the baby squirmed, and, in an agony of fear lest it should wake, he put it back again, while the perspiration rolled off of itself.

"Warm day," said Perkins, scratching his chin reflectively with his little finger. "Yes, I knowed you 'cause of them blue specticles. Blue specticles gives a man a uncommon and superior air."

Inwardly, but mildly, Professor Von Raab cursed his unfortunate spectacles.

"Did you see a woman running wildly about?" he asked slowly and solemnly.

"Well, not here," replied Perkins reflectively; "but I've seed a lot of 'em running about wild up to t'other station, gen'ally;" and the old man looked down ruminatingly, and pursed up his stubbly chin. "There's Miss Stiggin, **she** makes a pint of forgitting her umbril till the last minnit; and Miss Stott, that's Deacon Stott's wife, she allers loses one **of** her children, and **runs** about yellin' like the **town** crier. Then there's **them** that stops to inquire 'bout all other folks' relations, and what they've got in their markit-baskits, right on the brenk of eternity, with death a-whistlin' 'All aboard!' I've tuck **'em from under the** car-wheels more'n once, and never got so much as thankee for't."

"Is there a poor-house, or a foundling-asylum, **or** any place where I could leave this child?" asked the professor anxiously. Time was flying: he was due next morning at nine at his class.

"Lud, sir! you can't mean it. Why, you don't say it ain't yourn!"

The professor groaned in spirit.

"Don't I tell you somebody put it upon me?— a woman who looked as near crazy as any one out of Bedlam well could," he queried savagely, though his voice was suppressed almost to a whisper.

"Law, that's the way they alleys do, them

sort ; " and the wink that accompanied this irritat-
ing response nearly drove every rational thought
out of the professor's brain.   Whether to hurl the
unconscious baby at the head of that grim and oily
man, and fly, or apply his boot to the greasy habili-
ments, he hardly knew.

"Well, I wish you a pleasant journey, sir, you
and the little one.   Train's due in fifteen minutes,.
— gits in Tarryville two hours and a half — if
no accident happens.   No accident ain't happened
since it's been a road ; but lud, sir, there must
alleys be a fust time.   That's a fine-looking boy,
sir.   Good-by."

It was plain that the man was determined to
have his joke.   The professor also determined to
keep his temper — and the baby.   What else was
he to do for the time being ?   Plan after plan
came into his head, like lightning, and were re-
jected peremptorily.   Not a soul was in sight.
He peered anxiously up and down the dreary
road.   It was an utterly out-of-the-way place.
There would be no train after to-day till to-morrow at the same time.   What was he to do ?
Dinnerless, foot-sore, and perplexed, — he had
never in his life been in such a dilemma.   Perkins

had gone ; everybody had gone.   He might have been the only man in the world, for all he saw of humanity.

Something would not let him desert the help-less creature ; but what was he to do ultimately ? Confused thoughts of an asylum in his own city occurred to him.   Perhaps Providence would in-terpose.   Here came the train ; and with a vague trust in something, he scarcely knew what, he entered the car.

Chapter Four.

HE baby still slept. Gently the professor laid it down upon his knee, thinking of the time when he had cared for just such a helpless creature, motherless, and, but for him, altogether friendless.

In his mind's eye he saw a painted balcony, overhung by green vines; by his side a solitary rocking-chair, and a unique little bed made up on an old yellow settee, two faded footstools, and a camp-stool, composing the out-door furnishing of the place.

He could see himself sitting there with the patient baby-face looking up into his. He could see the dim outlines of the mountains, blue and gold and umber, bright, or black with cloud-shadows; the cool meadows lying at their feet; and nearer, a ledge of castle-like rocks with trees tall and slender, shooting from their brown fissures,

where one could find no royal heart of earth **to**
drop a seed in.

And the little German **rivers** shooting off here
and there, — blue as the June blue of heaven, —
and the little German bridges, their rough points
softened **by** distance into the seeming grace of
art, **though** they were simple rustic footholds —
how the past came rushing back upon him !

He was in the last car ; and taking off his spectacles he drew his hat, with that sheltering broad
brim, still farther over **his** brows. Thus shield-
ing himself as much as possible, he presently fell
into a reverie, and earth and all human belongings
fell away from him like a garment.

It was a full hour's ride to Tarryville. In fifteen minutes **by** the clock the baby stirred. Its
protector started, and suddenly came **back** to the
realities of life. The baby was actually staring at
him, with wide-open blue eyes. It was **a** refined
little face, albeit the lace and muslin that framed
it in were coarse and common in texture, and its
clothes were not certainly those of a babe of
quality. He looked around, and drew his **breath**
more freely, for they were all strangers. Then **he**
placed the baby **in a** more comfortable position,
and leaned **back** complacently.

At that moment a little gurgling sound, such as nothing but a baby can make, issued from the tiny red lips.

"Bless her little heart!" ejaculated a mild-eyed woman behind him — but she saw the baby. Women from almost any point of vision can see a baby.

"Dear me! it must be a girl," said the professor to himself.

"How old is she?" queried the woman, bending over.

"Well, a year or two, I guess," replied the poor man helplessly.

"You don't say!" and up went a pair of finely arched eyebrows. "How very small óf its age! Can it possibly be a year?"

"I — I might have missed a few months," responded the professor, wondering what he had said. "I don't — think I really can tell — what age exactly, babies are — when they — when" —

"When they are nursing, I suppose you mean," said the woman complacently.

"Yes, I — I guess that's it, exactly."

"Dear little thing! is its mother living?"

Here was a poser. Poor Prof. Raab devoted

nearly five minutes to the solution of this question, mentally.

"I have every reason to believe she is," he made reply, in his slow manner.

"Every reason to believe," cogitated the woman, who had begun to feel a peculiar interest in this mild-looking, large-eyed man. "Probably it's not his baby; but if not, why is it with him? Such a little thing ought not to travel without a mother, or nurse, or somebody."

The baby began an examination of its hands; then doubled them up, and launched out in a sort of free fight with nothing in particular.

For the moment the woman on the back seat had subsided; but the little one was too powerful a magnet.

She leaned forward, and watched it. Presently there were two tears trickling quietly down the channels of her cheeks.

"Sweet little thing!" she murmured, in a low, broken voice. "It makes me think of my own baby. It's your very image, sir."

"A-ahem!" choked the professor, crimson with indignation; and the baby came very near falling, in the eagerness with which its protector tugged at the window with one hand.

The atmosphere was close enough; but the poor dear woman at his back had forgotten her morning's repast of cucumbers and onions.

The baby by this time had one hand in his long silken, brown beard, and the other in his watch-chain, — a position that nothing in life but a baby could possibly achieve. While he was nervously trying to save his chain, which was an old heir-loom, and very slender, it suddenly occurred to him that the woman in the next seat was crying. Yes, she was surely wiping her eyes with a hand-kerchief. That sense which is situated in the back of the head, and answers for sight, and which in him was very strong, told him so. Presently she leaned forward, and chirruped to the little one, who was evidently making up her mind to a change in the programme. Goodness had become tire-some to her small faculties. The pleasant smile and clucking checked the serious down-curve of the crimson mouth, and she stared with rounder eyes and inarticulate gurgling at her admirer.

"It sets me to thinking of a dear little girl that I lost not long ago, sir, — the only one I ever had," said the woman, after a slight indulgence in infantile Latin with the absorbed baby. "It's very hard, sir, to lose them, — oh, it's very hard! One's home is so lonely! I've never felt the same woman since my baby died."

"My dear madam, won't you have this one?" queried the professor, a trifle more eagerly than he would have said, "Won't you have a slice of plum-pudding?" at dinner.

The woman started, looked at him with a puzzled wonder in her face that no pen can describe, and then subsided by degrees into her own corner.

"I can assure you, you are very welcome. It was a total stranger to me before to-day; put in my care by I don't know who, and probably never shall know: so you see, madam, the reason I offered it " —

"West Bend!" shouted the conductor; and thereupon the woman gathered up bags and bundles, and, with a look at the professor simply indescribable, lurched at and out of the open door; evidently bearing the impression away with her, that she had been conversing either with a madman or a child-stealer.

Chapter Five.

HE baby grew heavier and heavier. Its facial contortions were a study : it seemed simply resisting the conviction that it was time for a hearty cry, and mouthed, and tried to swallow its fists, both of them ; and finally, grown desperate by long battle with its small propensities, it burst into one sharp, terrific yell.

This was horrible. What mortal man could do in the way of handling a dissatisfied youngster, the professor did. He patted it on the back and chest indiscriminately ; he trotted it till it was black in the face ; he held it in every conceivable position. There were elements of disorder in progress with which he was not acquainted. Somebody lent him a helping hand and a handkerchief. The hand was motherly ; so was the face that met his, and that had taken the place of his talkative neighbor.

" Let me have **it,**" she said softly, and withdrew with her charge somewhere out of sight. The **professor** had a half-insane impression that **now was his** chance to escape. Should he fly from his torment, and essay a leap from the cars at the **next stopping-place?** Would it **be possible to mingle** with the crowd, and lose himself?

No: clearly the right thing was to face the responsibility, and do the **best** he could. The motherly-looking woman **re-appeared**: she wore a gently anxious look as she scrutinized the professor closely.

"It's very young to travel without a mother," she said softly.

"Yes, it is. About how old should you think it?" asked the professor eagerly.

"Well! **Upon my word!** Don't you know the age of your own child?" she questioned. "**Fa**-thers, **I** believe though, are generally ignorant **about** such matters," she added as she took her seat, the clatter of the cars almost drowning her voice. "Men, as a common thing, are utterly use-less in the management of babies. My husband isn't **the value of a** wood-saw in **his** own house. It'll sleep now, **I guess. My** own baby is only six months **old**; — and she was so hungry!"

"Upon what hypothesis, madam, do you venture the assertion that this is my child?" queried the professor with his profoundest expression.

The woman looked at him, dumb with consternation. Her lips parted, then closed again. She had experienced a sensation, and it was astonishingly like fear. Was the man crazy?

"Upon my word, I never saw such eyes in my life!" she muttered to herself, — "like red-hot steel."

Meantime the baby, after a succession of faint flourishes with its hands, and sundry feeble attempts at articulation of primitive Latin, and sufficient assertion with its feet to clear them of the dimity gown, exposing a row of pink pearls upon a waxen surface, submitted at last to its destiny, and fell fast asleep.

The poor little wretch! The miserable little nuisance! The tender, white-faced angel! Ah, now it smiled, and the silly heart of the professor melted within him. A voice that had often thrilled the inmost, finest tendrils of his soul seemed to be sounding in his ears, —

"You dear old goose!"

It had always been iterated with milk-white

winding arms about his neck, and soft kisses upon
his cheek. He felt very miserable and very foolish, and very happy altogether. It would never
do in the world to carry the baby there, would it?
Lissa and Miss Jo! what would they say? Well,
he could think it over; and he began to think.
Off and away flew that irrepressible thought, till
presently the baby was only a feather's weight
upon his knees. The formations of rock along
the route were remarkable. The granular lime-
stone, with its vein-like fissures and delicate coloring, set his ready mind to work upon calcareous
formations, crystals, fossil remains, and geognostic
phenomena. Pictures of beautiful landscapes followed each other in swift succession, — pictures
worthy of the genius of Claude Lorraine; but
over these he cast an absent eye. The rocks
pleased him better, with their vivid hues of crimson and yellow, — the hints of iron and of fire;
the rich, ruddy sandstone, broken into lace-work,
over which filtered here and there the divine tears
of nature, softening those rugged faces that told ·
their stories of neglect, of convulsions, of mighty
throes put in operation by the forces due to
man's genius. He had a passion for geology. He

had studied the mighty, sinuous masses of rock at
Elba, and the volcanoes of Stromboli, Vesuvius,
and Ætna. In the rich Saxon mines, he had
pored over the wonderful ores under the surface
of the earth; and he was now busy on the third
lecture of a series which he proposed giving in his
own city, and which had cost him months of study.

A sudden movement startled him. The baby
had rolled off his lap, and on to the floor; and,
probably much astonished by the sudden transition,
was swimming about helplessly on a dry surface,
and vainly striving to get its mouth free, in order
to give vent to its astonishment and indignation,
and which protest now escaped in a series of gasps.

"My sakes alive!" exclaimed a female voice;
and the woman opposite, witnessing the accident,
rushed upon the scene; and, stooping at the same
moment that he did, the concussion was inevitable.
The professor had a confused sense of artificial
flowers which scratched him, a pair of eye-glasses,
and a shower of small bundles; but between the
two they managed to lift the baby, dusty and
grimy from head to foot, and restore it, almost too
frightened to cry, to its original place. Everybody who could see, smiled, of course; and the

professor, who seemed to think the cars ought of their own accord to stop just now, and let him out, felt that the strangulation of that baby then and there would scarcely have been imputed as a crime; under the circumstances. The baby itself felt, no doubt, that the culminating point of its sufferings had been reached, and began to give its lungs free play.

" I'll take it again," said the motherly woman, and disappeared as before. The professor sighed savagely. Resentment filled his hitherto gentle breast. He felt like one in the clutches of a small relentless fiend. The child was an incubus. If it were only dark enough, he knew he should be tempted to throw it out of the car-window. But oh, strange illusion of human nature ! when the baby came again upon the scene, cleansed, encouraged, satisfied, and smiling, all its dimples in the old places, and actually held out its little fat hands to him as if claiming protection, the soft, foolish heart was wax again, though he would have given worlds to rid himself of the incumbrance.

" Won't you keep it, ma'am ? " he asked anxiously. " You're a mother, and you know how to deal with them. It may be somebody would take it off your hands."

"Really, sir, I don't understand you," said the motherly woman. "I have done as much for a strange child, I think, as I am called to do."

"So have I," ruefully sighed the professor.

"Do you wish to give your child away? Is its mother dead? If so, sir, I consider you an unnatural father, — an unnatural father, sir;" and her eyes burned under her spectacles. "As for me, I have brought up ten, and my youngest is only six months; and none of them on the bottle, — no, sir, not one."

"We'll — we'll change the subject," said the professor, with a weak smile. "I — I've rather a remote acquaintance with the milky way: of course I refer to the nebulous stars, averaging from the tenth to the eleventh degree of magnitude; and " —

"Tarryville!" cried the conductor.

"I really believe," muttered the professor, as he carefully lifted the baby, — "I really believe I made a pun — and I hate puns."

"Is that man foolish, or crazy?" queried the motherly woman of her neighbor.

"I know he gave me a dreadful bump," was the response, with a gesture of pain.

A tender twilight was coming on. The professor had buttoned up his coat, in the car, to the very throat, and tied his yellow bandanna about his chin. He now drew his broad-brimmed hat much lower, till he nearly concealed his eyebrows. Fortunately there were but four people who left the cars, none of them familiar to him. The baby was still asleep. He passed the depot with his head averted, and looking out as sharply as he could, with his uncertain eyes, that he ran into nobody. As he approached the more densely populated parts of the town, his courage failed him. Half blind and half angry, he reproached himself and fate. Suppose, in spite of his effort at a disguise, somebody should know him! He had a class of girls in German, — keen, fun-loving creatures, who had steadily endeavored always to get the better of him. And even if he reached home, and told the truth, and all that, there was a certain flavor of the ludicrous about the whole affair, which would cling to his garments forever. He began walking wildly and unsteadily forward, lost in thought. One street looked much the

same to him as another, without his glasses. He
was not quite sure where he was: he felt jaded,
dispirited, and wearied, from his long tramp all
day among the hills; and he seemed to feel the
weight of the specimens in his pocket, pulling him
down; and the baby grew heavier and heavier.
Lights began to twinkle in the houses; he heard
the clatter of dishes now and then, with the delicate clink of glass. A savory smell delighted his
nostrils. He looked at the baby: it still slept.

"It may be a temptation of Satan," he said to
himself; "but the flesh is weak." He ran up the
steps of a house, hap-hazard, deposited the baby
tremblingly, rang the bell enough almost to rouse
the dead; then sprang backward, performing the
feat of tumbling over himself twice, and ran up
the street, down another, doubling and winding,
till he was blocks away, and had leisure to stop and
draw one long, relieved breath.

Untying his handkerchief, lifting his hat, unbut-
toning his coat, and putting on his second eyes,
he felt that Richard was himself again. He
threw out his arms, so long burdened with that
small but terrible weight. He realized his freedom, and felt no compunctions of conscience, like

sharp-tongued **spectres, rise in his** bosom. **He**
walked **on towards** the river.   **There** was still light
enough to see the **glossy surface** of its faint-blue
level in the dead calm, the reflection of the opposite shore, the **twinkle of** gray that the trees let
in **of** the evening **sky** not yet in shadow ; **a** boat
here and there, propelled by **lazily** plashing **oar ; a**
dim, red-shirted figure, bending low to the water's
edge.

"I'll go home **by** a circuitous route," he said
smilingly : "they know my habits ; and I'll say
nothing about my little adventure, though **it** will
burn on **my** tongue, for **I** always tell Lissa every
thing."

Chapter Six.

E were still talking about the baby, and wondering what was best to be done.

"Do you know what will be said?" I asked. "Why, my dear, it will get in all the papers, and I shall have a nice time of it in 'The Regulator.'"

"What possibly can be said to your injury?" asked Lissa innocently.

"Well, my political enemies might make a handle of it to tease me, or rival papers get hold of it. But suppose we go down and look at the young Ishmaelite," I said; and forthwith the procession formed, I at the head, Lissa grasping my coat-flaps, and Jo, shaking that sentimental ringlet, bringing up the rear.

"Vow to *my* grief!" exclaimed Tiddy, as we entered the dining-room in solemn expectancy, "it's got almos' all its teef." The child lay upon her knees, carefully smoothed out ; and a bottle close by gave evidence that **Tiddy** had had her **own** experience **with hungry children.** It was so bright, so pretty, so trustful in its unconsciousness, that **my** own heart warmed a little as **I** contemplated it in silence.

"**Why,** Carlos mine, it's a little beauty," cried **Lissa,** bending over the dimpled face that laughed **in hers.**

"**De** Lord's **gub** it nice **eyes,**" said Tiddy contemplatively, **with** that inward chuckle **peculiar** to the negro.

"**O** Jo! wouldn't she look lovely in a fine jaconet muslin trimmed with valenciennes?" cried Lissa, with renewed ecstasy.

"And a **blue** sack of the thinnest zephyr," added Jo. "*Isn't* she sweet?"

"**My dear, it's** a boy," said I. "That extraordinary development in **front of** the temples **promises well for his** future excellence in intellectual attainments."

Old Tiddy gave me one look, — it was almost contemptuous, — turned **her face aside, and tossed** her gray old head.

"Well, *ef* it's a boy," she said, "**den de** Lord's

made a big mistake. You can call her Jim ef you will, but I sh'd call her Dinah ef she was my color."

I bowed before woman's superior wisdom.

"O Charlie! *may* I keep her?" and the look I never could resist was turned towards me.

"I can't consent that you should take so much care and trouble: you don't know any thing about it," was my answer.

"But *I* do, brother Charlie: I've taken care of children. Lissa may consider it a plaything; I'll take all the care of it: I've nothing else to do," was Jo's plea.

"And we'll have a nurse, you know," echoed Lissa.

"But what will people say?"

Lissa turned, and gave me a curious look.

"I thought I haf my husband who cares not for Mrs. Grundy!" she said, in her delicious brogue, and with flashing eyes. "What would Heaven say when you pass by on the other side? *I* would be the *good* Samaritan, and care nothing of all at the world!"

She looked glorious as she spoke thus, and I own I felt correspondingly foolish; though why,

in all the States of Columbia, I should take and
do for this young stranger, was more than I could
understand.

"Its parents may be very improper people," I
added, anxious to try her further.

"So much the better for her, if she fall into
goot hands," said my wife steadily.

"Are you really in earnest, Lissa? And you,
Jo, are you willing to take the responsibility of
nourishing and cherishing this young castaway?"

"Cow's milk an' cracklings," murmured Tiddy,
in a reverie. "Laws, you ken brung up a chile
a'mos' on nuthin. It's de mental fuss an' de cal-
culashun dat tells on de sperrit. De Lord grows
'em right along."

"I'm willing to try," said Jo meditatively.

"'We can keep it a while, you know, and see,"
said Lissa, carefully placing her words.

"Then the court is willing," was my response.
"What are you going to do with the youngster
while we eat supper?"

"I'll tote it in my room, and put it to bed," said
Tiddy, cuddling the infant in her capacious arms,
and leaving the trio alone.

"Jo, we'll have a nice little nursery in the third

story," said Lissa, "just as we **do in Germany.**"
And she poured out the tea after her usual laugh-
ing fashion, while I passed **round the biscuits** for
which our old Tiddy was famous.

"**I don't** know why we should particularly want
a German nursery," said Jo, who was intensely
patriotic. "American customs are good enough
for me, *I* **should say**" — And here she paused
with a wry face, while the curl on her forehead
quivered sympathetically.

"I hope there will be no difference of opinion,"
said I, biting into my biscuit; and there *I* stopped,
with the morsel **between my** teeth, and a queer
quiver **of the** facial muscles.

Lissa by this time had tasted her tea; a little
cry escaped her, and she shuddered from head **to
foot.**

"**I** hope **it** isn't a case of wholesale poisoning,"
was my first remark.

"**The** baby couldn't certainly have done it,"
laughed Jo, I almost **thought** maliciously.

"It's in the biscuit too," I said, **as, tasting my**
tea, I made a worse face than before, and shook
my head.

"What can Tiddy have been thinking about?"

queried Lissa pettishly: "she is getting too old to cook. Try the cake: that was baked this afternoon."

"Sugared with salt, just the same," I said, after sniffing at the rich-looking loaf.

"My dear Lissa, if I were you I would *never* come into the kitchen," said Jo mildly.

"Why! what have I to do with it?" queried Lissa, her lips quivering. "I don't cook."

"No; but you *would* put the things into boxes this noon, you know, and you probably put the sugar in the salt-box: there's no other way of accounting for it."

"I'm always doing something wrong," murmured my wife, looking at me appealingly.

"You're always doing something unique, I'll allow," I said, laughing; "but it's nothing so very dreadful. If Tiddy had just tasted " —

"But she never does taste," said Lissa, gathering the cake and biscuit together: "I wish we had somebody that did."

"Don't trouble yourself, dear: let me call Tiddy. Oh! I forgot," and I assumed as demure an expression as I could call up: "she's got that baby."

"It doesn't hurt to wait upon myself," said

Lissa, carefully guarding her speech. "You know we shall have a nurse-girl " —

"To wait upon," I added significantly. My wife looked a little cross; but she and Jo cleared the table, brought on some old bread and new preserves, and just as we prepared to taste the tea dashed with its proper elements, a peculiar ring sounded at the door.

"Conrad, dear old fellow!" exclaimed Lissa.

"The professor!" said Jo, with a slight infusion of red in her cheeks. I had noticed before that she always colored at sound of his step, or if he came unexpectedly.

"I'll let him in," said I, "as Tiddy is busy with *the baby.*" There was a mellow emphasis about the last of my sentence, that made Lissa frown and shrug her shoulders, and call me a bear; but I went sturdily up stairs, like a man conscious of having the truth on his side, and let the professor in.

Chapter Seben.

E told the story of the salted supper with great glee. The professor laughed merrily, and declared that hot biscuit was bad for the digestion, and that for his part, though he always ate it when it was set before him, he was very glad of the more wholesome cold bread.

I had never seen my good friend and brother Conrad in better spirits. He was really, as Lissa said afterwards, jolly. Every thing pleased him, and he praised and ate the preserves extravagantly.

Splendid time ! Lectured to a large house — vote of thanks, and fifty dollars. Meant to bring Lissa some fruit or flowers, but (here he played a little nervously with his fork) he staid so late in his geological researches, that — that it wasn't really possible. Fine country up there, splendid rocks ; reminded him of Germany more than any

place he had been in. Liked the people — ahem!
that is, he hadn't seen much of the people; and
then he inquired in a roundabout way if Lissa
had met any of his friends.

"Of course you mean Miss Walters," laughed
Lissa, while Jo put down her cup hastily.

Miss Walters was the daughter of the dean of
the university; a splendid girl, not beautiful, but
with a face sufficiently striking to attract the attention at once. Hers was a lovely and most lovable
character, and in the German class she invariably
carried off the honors. We thought, Lissa and I,
that Conrad was in love with her. He watched
her lips when she spoke: there was a certain indefinable tenderness in the way he pronounced her
name, and little germ-hints in his reveries, sufficiently strong to give Lissa the clew to his
thoughts. And Miss Walters did not seem averse
to his attentions. He walked home with her sometimes from lectures; and the dean was very particular and precise, and seldom allowed any one the
pleasure of his daughter's society, for she was his
only child and like the very apple of his eye.

"I mean — any of my friends," said the professor cheerfully, "Miss Walters among them, of

course;" and he blushed a little, and very graciously
offered Miss Jo the bread-plate, which she de-
clined, as there was no bread in it.   There was no
use in his begging pardon: everybody laughed,
though there was a little vexed look between my
sister's eyebrows, and I knew from that moment
that she was no friend to Miss Walters.

"Conrad, do you know, dear, that this is your
fourth cup?" asked Lissa archly.

"Ah, yes, but I am so thirsty!   I had a hard
walk of it to-day, — yes, a very hard walk; and I
went without my dinner too, but that you know
is nothing."

"Without your dinner!" cried Lissa, "and not
a bit of hearty food on the table.   Dear me! Tiddy
must get some cold meat immediately.   Call
Tiddy, somebody."

"My dear, you forget that Tiddy is engaged,"
I said in my softest and slowest tone.   A look of
annoyance crossed Lissa's expressive countenance,
but she was equal to the emergency.

"Oh, yes! I did forget," she responded with a
significant gesture, which meant, "Don't tell Conrad just yet."   "But I know where the meat is.
Come, Charlie, the ice-chest is for me too much;"
and off I went like a big boy at her beck.

"I don't know what to speak to Conrad, — how to explain it, I mean," she said gravely, as I lifted the heavy lid, and she deftly carved a few thin slices of cold mutton. "I wish that thoughtless fellow had got his dinner. Tiddy saved this for breakfast. You men are so much alike!"

"Yes, we are something on the same pattern, I suppose," I rejoined; "but why don't you want to let Conrad know about the baby?"

"Well, simply for the reason, I suppose, that he will laugh at me."

"Aha! who is afraid of the world now?" said I triumphantly.

"But Conrad is not the world, don't you see? if it was anybody but Conrad, I wouldn't care." She held the plate of meat in one hand, and had taken up the candle, poising it at such an angle, unconsciously, that she made of herself one of the finest Rembrandt-paintings in flesh and blood that I had ever seen, more exquisite than any in the galleries of Europe.

"What are you looking at me for so?" she asked as I stood transfixed.

"I was only wishing I were an artist, and could take the light and shadow of your face just now," I made reply.

"Nonsense! You will do what Conrad failed to do," she said, blushing, — "spoil me, if you praise me so much."

"But how do you know I was praising you? I only spoke of lights and shadows."

"Then you didn't think it was pretty?" she said naïvely. It was so much like a woman!

"No, I thought it was beautiful," was my response, with a kiss that nearly put out the candle —for we used that primitive light when we went through the passages, as the ell of the house was new, and as yet had no gas-fixtures put in.

Conrad protested against the trouble, but ate his cold meat with an appetite. Suddenly a strange sound saluted our ears. It was an infantile scream, and a lusty one.

"The baby is crying!" exclaimed Lissa with an expression I feel it impossible to describe.

"The baby! what baby?" and Conrad laid down knife and fork, and it seemed as if all the color went out of his face.

Enter Tiddy, her turban awry, her face flushed with that peculiar hue which denotes trouble in the sable soul, her neckerchief torn and otherwise disturbed, her forehead and mouth puckered and quivering.

"Ef dis yer chile hasn't got a small debble inside o' her, den I ain't a baptized Christian," said poor Tiddy, and then stopped breathless. The change to a brilliant light worked wonders; the small woman stopped, and began looking round out of eyes rimmed with large salt-water brilliants, till it seemed as if her glance fastened itself on the professor. As for him, his eyes grew large, and his forehead paler and paler.

"Well," he panted, "I — I'm surprised. I — I'm astonished. I — I may say — I'm haunted," he added in a curiously changed voice, and his hands trembled as he wiped the perspiration from his temples.

"Hy, 'fessor!" exclaimed Tiddy, her wrinkled brow clearing up a little as she began tossing the baby. "I's glad ter see yer home, an' so's this blessed baby, I reckon."

"Wha — what? Wher — where did you get it?" gasped the professor, rising and steadying himself; then, catching himself up with a haggard smile, "It — it's a queer sight in this house."

"Some man's been done gone sot dat ar' chile on de steps, an' den he flew," said the old woman with characteristic gestures, pawing the air with her unoccupied arm, and looking like an animated wind-mill.

"How do you know it was **a man?**" I asked, eying my friend Conrad with some surprise : "Did you **see** him?" Conrad **turned** away abruptly.

"**Man** must 'a' put it dar, shore, 'cause man **don't kar** what becomes o' this yer sort gin'ly. **Didn't see God** lookin' right down on him, reckon."

They were all intent upon the baby, and it was well. I saw, without seeming to, that Conrad staggered as he moved, and his face was certainly a study.

"Conrad, are you sick?" asked Lissa, suddenly turning round.

"Not **at** all, **but** very tired," he replied quietly. "**I believe I'll go to** my room." She went up to **him with a** good-night kiss, and threw her arms **about his neck.**

"Would you keep it, Conrad, the poor little forsaken thing?" she asked. "I know you will say yes."

"**Of** course," he responded feebly.

"You dear old goose!" and there was a rapturous hug.

"Conrad says yes, without an if or an and," said Lissa, turning to me as he left the room; only she said it in the most curiously broken language which I cannot render here, her way of saying it making its chiefest charm.

Chapter Eight.

T must have been eleven o'clock when Lissa graciously accorded me her company that night. For full two hours she had been trotting between my room and Jo's, bringing me accurate reports of the situation, and at last assuring me that the baby was asleep for the night. I hoped so, but doubted it.

A light knock at the door confirmed my fears. Lissa had retired ; but I fully expected a message from the infantile side of the house.

A haggard face met my gaze : it was Conrad, in his dressing-gown, his hair brushed from his forehead, his expression uncanny.

" I came down to ask you up into my room. Is Lissa asleep ? "

" I don't think she is," I replied.

" Can you come up for a few moments ? I have something to tell you."

His manner was so earnest and solemn, that I felt a thrill of dread tingle through my nerves.

"Certainly I can come, though it is rather late," I said.

"I know it, but I won't keep you long." So I told Lissa I was going up stairs with Conrad, and would be back soon ; then I followed him on tip-toe, warned by Lissa, as I left, *not to wake the baby.* I am afraid I said, "Confound the baby!" with unnecessary vehemence, even under my breath. As I passed Jo's room, I know I knocked over a pyramid consisting of waiters, cans, and goblets, sufficient to rouse a whole orphan-asylum ; and that further, the professor's dressing-gown, catching in some other surreptitious article, dragged it clattering for what seemed a mile of drugget, bringing us both up standing, and looking at each other with rising hair, and that expression of mingled terror and malignity which fortunately can be substituted for something worse. "For out of the mouth of man cometh" — you know the quotation, — especially when he is grieved at his heart.

We gained Conrad's room at last, a pleasant student's apartment, bright with choice books, chiefly his German collection, where his flute-stand and music-rack, guitar and foils, had each their appropriate place ; Lissa's taste having contrived a recess for the bed, which was curtained off from the rest of the room. Conrad gravely shut the door, locked it carefully, placed two chairs opposite each other, and gravely beckoned me to seat myself.

With a feeling that some dread incantation was about to be inaugurated, I sat down facing him.

"You will be astonished to learn," he said, — the tassel of his study-cap throwing a portentous shadow over his nose, — "that — _I_ left that baby upon your doorstep."

I don't think a cannon-ball passing within an inch of my left temple would have more completely stunned me out of my self-possession. I could only draw back in my chair and look at him. I suppose I said with some emphasis, —

"You !".

Though I was not really conscious of having spoken, for he answered, —

"Yes, I; and I count it an almost miraculous coincidence; for, I assure you, I didn't mean it."

"But, my dear fellow," said I, "where in the name of wonder, did you get it ?"

He began to tell his story, and I began to laugh. Not even the thought of that sleeping cherub down stairs restrained me. I saw him blundering about without his glasses. I followed the fortunes of that unhappy baby with smothered throes, until he came to the place where his courage failed him, and he wandered about the streets with which ordinarily he was familiar, like a blind man. Then, as I saw him deliberately place the unconscious Arab on his own doorstep, the ecstasy culminated : I silently went down on my knees, and then I rolled and laughed, and laughed and rolled, till I brought down the music-stand, with all its accompaniments, upon my head, while the professor stood protesting and laughing alternately, declaring that I would wake up the household, and adding, with tears in his eyes, that he didn't see as it was any matter to be merry over.

A knock at the door, which brought me to my senses. I opened it, and there stood Lissa, curiously involved in her double shawl, and pale as any ghost.

. "My dear!" I cried, in consternation.

. "I heard such dreadful noises; and then I dreamed that you and Conrad were fighting one of those miserable German duels. Of course I was very foolish, as I always am, and dreadfully frightened."

"You silly child! The idea of my fighting with Conrad! We had a little business together: that was all," I said, screwing my mouth up; and then I turned to him.

"Not a word, yet a while," I muttered in an undertone: "keep your secret, and I will keep mine. Good-night;" and we parted. I left Lissa at Jo's door, going just to look at baby; and I didn't see her again that night, for no sooner did my head touch the pillow than I was asleep; and though I wake tolerably late, — just in time generally to see my wife putting on the finishing touches at the mirror, — I failed to hear the first rustle, or catch the light of eyes watching for me, the next morning.

I did not see much of the baby that day. Lissa walked herself into a fever in search of a nurse; and I found myself confronted by a moon-faced young lady of French extraction, extravagantly attired, when I returned from the office.

"We want a *nice*-looking nurse, you know," said Lissa; "and so few will wear the real *bonne* cap!"

"What do you give her for her nice looks, my love?" I asked, pleased to see her pleased.

"Only twenty dollars a month."

"My child!" I exclaimed, aghast. "Do you know that is nearly twice as much as we give our cook Tiddy?"

"Why, I could hardly get her to come, because we kept not a carriage," was Lissa's reply.

"So she expected to be taken an airing every day or two, did she? What that baby will cost us!"

Lissa drew back a little petulantly.

"If it cannot afforded be, then I will send her away," she said.

"It shall be afforded, mine vrow, if it pleases you," I said. "It is to be presumed that this young lady will mature as fast as others of her species; that is, that all traces of childhood will have vanished by the time she attains her fifth year, and she will begin to attitudinize for the benefit of the young gentlemen hereabouts."

"You do make every thing into fun," she said, her face still clouded.

"Not you, my darling: I never make fun of you, whatever you do."

"And — and you won't scold, if I tell you there is something else?"

"Of course not. What is it, — a new bib and tucker?"

"A — a baby-carriage."

"Oh!" and visions of new and expensive nursery furniture floated in blue and gold through my imagination.

"Yes: I went up to Locke's, because that you told me never to go but to the very *best* places; and it is such a beauty!"

"I dare say," I responded gravely.

"With the dearest little white-satin curtains, that draw at the back, and don't not let the sun in at the least."

"Do not, my dear," I corrected.

"Yes, do not let no sun in at all."

"Don't let *any* sun in."

"Yes, don't let not *any* sun in: that is what I meant to say," she went on excitedly, her eyes sparkling, and her cheeks brightening, so that I entirely forgot my surprise in contemplating her beauty.

"And what did the carriage cost?"

"Why, I think," and she scrutinized the carpet,

— " I think he said he would take under ten dollars
for cash."

" Ah ! you mean take off."

" Yes, yes; take off, and let me have it for
seventy-five dollars."

It was rather steep, considering I was unwill-
ingly called upon to do the duty of a step-father;
but I kept my temper, and mused in silence for
the space of a minute and a half.

"And then"— she broke the silence, — a dead
pause again — "I got the bathing-tub."

"My dear," said I explosively, " there are bathing-tubs in the house, extremely fine ones, that
cost me a mint of money."

"But not bathing-tubs for a baby," she said
quickly.

Oh, that wife of mine !

"No; that is very true," I said quietly. "I
didn't allow for the baby when I put them in."

"Besides, if we are going to have a nursery,
we must have things a little suitable to it. And
so I bought a chair, and some jingles, and rubber
for its teeth to gnaw on like a little mouse ; but
they will all be here in a short, small time, then
you shall see them."

I put on a pair of mental spectacles of the largest magnifying power, and took my wife by the hand.

"You are the most charming woman in the world," I said; "but at the same time, allow me the liberty of adding, the completest little fraud that ever a good-natured man was humbugged by;" and I surveyed her with my sweetest smile.

"Frod," she ejaculated. "What's a frod? Charlie, are you making fun at me?"

"No, my dear. I am not making fun at you, or of you; but I wish you to look at this matter in the light of sober common sense. This is not our child. No amount of dressing, or caring for, or spending, will make it our child."

"It is God's child," she said in a quavering, solemn little voice.

"Ahem! well, that may be," I said, clearing my throat. "Undoubtedly there is some truth in your assertion, if not more; but at the same time it is only thrown upon our hands for the present. Don't you see, it may be claimed by somebody."

She shook her head.

"The child's mother may be living."

"Oh, no, no! Mothers only leave their children when they die. No *living* mother could do *so!*"

"We don't know: there may have been reasons, powerful reasons, — hunger, distress."

"I would die with it, then! I would die with it!" she cried passionately.

What would you have done, reader, with that wife of mine — that is, if she had been your wife? Actually the words stuck in my throat, and, with some other indefinable sensation, produced such a choking that I let silence do duty for speech for a considerable period. I don't mind saying that things danced about somewhat, through the mist that happened in my eyes just at that period, including Lissa, who seemed indulging in a remarkable kind of polka, now here, now there. At last — I hated to do it, but tears running down at a man's nose, you know, have a ridiculous effect, — and so I took out my handkerchief, and, pretending to sneeze, rubbed my eyes dry.

"Lissa," said I, looking serious without the least effort, and speaking with editorial brevity, "that baby is yours. I give you *carte blanche* to any extent save absolute ruin. Amen."

Chapter Nine.

F **course** people talked. That hydra head **set all its** tongues wagging. Not that we heard what was **said**; but a baby-carriage **and a** French nurse, and a doctor's chaise every second day, and a new girl for the door-bell, — all these at one and the same period, with no premonitions before, and no explanations after (except to a select few), were assuredly sufficient cause, even **in a** comparatively new neighborhood, to awaken and stimulate curiosity to an unlimited **extent.**

We made no particular mystery about it, merely saying to special friends that **it** had been put in our charitable keeping, leaving our neighbors to find out for themselves by whom, if they could.

Meantime the baby lived like **a** queen's child and an heir to **the** throne. **It was an** exceptionally good-tempered little thing, always rosy and

dimpled, always ready to be tossed and tumbled;
and though I could not for the life of me feel any
thing more than a friendly and wish-it-well sort of
interest, still, as I had to foot the bills, and they
were occasionally, to state it mildly, rather startling, the baby's presence in the household was
something more than a myth, even though I seldom
took the pains to make a more intimate acquaintance with her ladyship.

I am sorry to say that sometimes I secretly
anathematized the baby, with emotions that scarcely do credit to one's Christianity. It was on occasions when I was ruthlessly awakened from some
happy dream by a draught of cold air, to learn
that my wife had *only* run in to see if Jo had covered the baby up well, and with sweet and serene
consciousness didn't know why I should care, —
she had only been gone a minute.

Or when, in the dark of the morning, busy over
my cogitations on some editorial, I was startled to
see a ghost in a long white gown gliding over the
carpet, — the light so dim as to half-etherealize
every object, — with a nurse-lamp in one hand,
and a spoon in the other, the small flame throwing
those rich shadows, that, on my wife's face, always

culminated in some new beauty.   And yet I could never bring myself to chide her for these night wanderings, since she appeared to take such pleasure in them.   I always seemed to behold her pleading for some divine right vested in that child, by virtue of its simple humanity.   I always heard the sweet, low, tremulous assertion, —

"It is God's child."

And so I held my peace.

"Do you know," she said to me one day, "I am almost more pleased on Jo's account than on my own, that we kept the baby?"

"And why?" I asked naturally.

"Because she is happier."

"She seemed happy enough before," I made reply.

"Ah! you do not know: you men never see any thing," she said with a mournful shake of the head.

"Perhaps I see more than you think."

"What! have you found it out?   Poor, dear Jo!"

"Possibly I have," I said at a venture.

"And you don't think Conrad sees it?"

"No," I answered contemplatively, "I don't think he does."

"Then don't you ever make one small hint to him ; because now, you see, the baby takes up her mind."

What was my wee wife driving at ? I puzzled my brains in vain to find a clew to her meaning. Had Jo learned of Conrad's complicity with our small domestic institution ? No : that could not be it.

"You see, it may not be the best ; but it does happen at some times. The first that I saw of you, — the very first, — my heart went out to you. If you had gone away and left me, not knowing, the world had been so dark ! "

Ah ! I caught her meaning. Jo, my mature and sentimental sister, fancied herself in love with the professor. Or it may have been no fancy. Conrad's tender, woman-like ways ; Conrad's dark, fathomless eyes, beautiful even under those unromantic glasses ; his always gentle and almost lover-like devotion to all women with whom he was thrown in social contact, — had doubtless led her to believe that he was more interested in her than the dictates of mere friendship warranted.

I was a little astonished to see old Tiddy, not long after, rush into the room with eyes rolling, and hands flying.

"I vow to my rest, Mars' Charlie, dem ar' two wimen-folks jis' quarril dar eyes out over dat ar' chile."

"Quarrel! what do you mean, Tiddy? My wife never quarrels," I said sternly.

"Maybe she don't, then," said Tiddy savagely. "Gineral times she's sweet as loaf-sugar b'iled down; but when she gits the old scratch in her, thar ain't a bar'l vinegar in old Jarsey that'll beat her for souriness: dat's Hebben's trufe. She won't let dat ar' chile go to sleep in de ole-fashioned way, ordered by de Lord hisself, fur's I know."

"Tiddy, if I hear you talk disrespectfully of your mistress, I'll send you down South," I said.

"Mout's well. She's little, Miss Lissa is, — I'll 'low that; but when she put her han' on my shoulder, case I sided wid de Lord's way, I jest spinned out; an' Miss Jo got crying; dat's de gospil fact, I vow to my rest."

Was it possible that Lissa had so far forgotten herself as to push the old negress out of the room?

"Did your mistress strike you?" I asked.

"She put her han' on me, and I spinned out. I's too old to be pushed, — make my oath on dat."

I wended my way to the nursery very reluctantly.

There sat Jo by the empty cradle,—it had cost a good deal of money too,—looking, especially about the eyes, like a much-injured woman. Lissa, her little face set like stone, stood by a crib which had some way got there without my knowledge,— a recent purchase, no doubt; and on the pretty embroidered coverlet lay the child, sobbing, and evidently trying to assert its will, while Lissa held it down with one hand.

"What is the trouble?" I asked impatiently.

"Lissa will let the baby cry itself to death," said Jo, wiping her eyes with her handkerchief.

"I shall train this child as it ought to be trained," said Lissa firmly. "It is crying for the cradle."

"Well, isn't that the right place for a baby?" I asked.

"Yes, it is; and I should have rocked it asleep an hour ago," said Jo with a sob in her voice.

"Yes; and it would always depend upon your rocking," retorted Lissa. "I have been reading a very wise paper, and it gives good reasons against rocking children. It hurts their heads, and it hurts their spines."

"But I was rocked, and Jo was rocked, and you were rocked. I don't know that we are cerebrally weak, or have **any defect in our** spines, on that **account."**

"That's **what I told her,"** said Jo.

"I don't mean this **baby will be rocked,"** said Lissa, firm as **the hills.**

"But, Lissa," **said I,** "**do be** reasonable " —

"March right straight out of this room, both of **you,"** said Lissa, coming up to **us** flashing like a **small** park **of artillery.** Jo actually ran, but I stood the fire for **a moment.**

"Lissa," **I said,** softly, "**I** shall **leave** you — to your **own** reflections ; " and walked off grenadier-fashion, with an imaginary ramrod down my back. Then I stood outside of the door ; at **one** moment boiling over with resentment, the next exploding with laughter. That wife of mine had fairly routed me, had proclaimed herself master of me **and all ; and** even the baby was succumbing **to her** imperious will, for as I stood there its sobbings **gradually ceased. I** would have given much to open the door, and witness what was going on, but my pride prevented that.

Not long after, Conrad came **in.**

"Well, Mr. Professor," said **I,** "**you** made a **very fair** soldier of that **wife of mine.** She has besieged the fortress in good style ; conquered the enemy, driven out her husband and her husband's sister, and stands upon the ramparts a victorious general. How do you manage these things in Germany? Shall I own myself put in subjection by my wife?"

"I never knew her to do such a thing," he said, as I related the facts from a humorous point of view.

"Then the baby has demoralized her, and I have a very great mind to send it to — Jericho."

Something came softly behind me ; two arms were folded on my back ; and, as I fancied, somebody's face was laid on the arms, and, as I *knew*, somebody was sobbing softly and repentantly. It was a queer position, and I didn't dare to laugh, and so disturb the solemnity of the picture. I had had my back taken by reporters on very rare occasions ; but to be wept upon by a small woman, was a decidedly novel sensation, and I was careful not to disturb the position till I had had my revenge.

"Have you seen that superb picture," I asked Conrad, "'When a man's single, he lives at his ease'?"

"No, I have not," was the professor's reply, his eyes twinkling.

"It gives one half a longing for a bachelor's life," I went on relentlessly, — "all ease and contentment, nobody to please but himself, no indulgences to buy "—

The sobbing continued.

"Hadn't you better come round on the other side, little woman?" I queried, as Conrad went out laughing softly to himself. "I'm all ready to ask you to forgive me."

There was an impetuous rush, and a restrained cry of, "O Charlie!"

"Is the baby asleep, my dear?"

"O Charlie!"

"Shall we sell the cradle?" I whispered, smoothing the pretty hair that clung like gold-thread to my breast.

"No — sell the crib! I've been harsh and cruel: I didn't know it was in me to be so cruel. Tell Jo to rock the baby to sleep, — poor old Jo! it's all her comfort; but she's so cross sometimes! And you'll forgive me, won't you?"

"Well, I had a sort of hazy impression that it was my place to ask forgiveness: how is it?"

"I hate myself, that's how it is; but please don't laugh; scold me, but don't laugh. Where is poor Tiddy? I've got to ask her pardon, too, or I'm afraid she'll poison me."

I had to laugh outright now.

"That's a moderately selfish motive, mine vrow," I said caressingly.

"Did you drive her out of the room too?"

"I have been very bad indeed," was the whispered reply.

"Where did you learn your tactics, my brave soldier?"

"I'm not brave: I'm a coward; and, if you talk to me so, you'll — break my heart."

"Then shall we kiss and make up?"

She held her lips to mine.

"And shall I disgrace myself by confessing that I never admired you so much in my life?"

"And I never hated myself so much," she said, downcast.

"It all comes of the baby."

"Oh, no, no! don't say that: let us love it the little while it stays."

"The little while?"

"Perhaps."

"Why do you talk that way, Lissa?" I asked
anxiously.

"Because I have seen it in dreams, so often;
and it always looked like something different, —
an angel."

"Lissa, are you superstitious? do you believe
in dreams? I detest such fallacies: my wife must
be above them."

"Yes, I do believe in dreams: I dreamed of
you before I saw you."

"Impossible, child!"

"But I did: I remember of it perfectly."

"And what was your dream?"

"Oh! it was very simple. I thought I was pick-
ing currants in our garden — you recall that dear
garden?"

"I do perfectly: I wish we had such a one
here."

"Ah, well! it took hundreds of years to grow up
to that. There arn't such gardens to be seen in
this new country. So I picked the currants for a
pie, — Gretchen made such currant pies! such
ones as I will make some day, — when I happened
to look up. You know the wall where it seems as
if the sun shines, even in the days of dark, just in

the opening of the apple-trees ? Yes : well, there
I saw a man with a book in his hand ; and I wondered and wondered who it could be, for it looked
not of my country. And above this man, like a
soft veil of some shining mist, there stood somebody bending over, and it seemed to be pointing
to me. I grew a little frightened, and let the currants fall out of my lap, bowl and all; and you
came along so slowly, step by step, and you
picked up the bowl of currants, and said, —

" 'I then have found thee !' "

" But how do you know it was me?"

" Because I do. It was your face, though to be
sure the features were a little clouded; but you
needn't laugh, it was you ! "

The little woman was standing now against a
table, an almost spiritual light playing over her
earnest face, and, as every new phase did, impart-
ing a novel charm to her countenance. Her arms
were folded, the sleeves lightly falling back; her
eyes seemed reading from some unseen page. I
felt myself strangely moved.

" And the other form?" I said, "was it a
woman ? "

" I thought it so," she made answer.

"And what did she do?" I asked a little nervously.

" She smiled, oh, so beautiful! and, as she smiled, melted away."

Superstitious, given to dreams, wilful, womanly, angelic! What wonder I exclaimed with a husband's transport, though with the sceptical horror of .an old newspaper man, —

"Oh, that wife of mine!"

Chapter Ten.

A LETTER from Jack!

I threw down the rest of the mail, and was soon lost in an ecstatic vision of my friend's new home in Santa Barbara, for every line sparkled with light and color.

Jack and Lina had emigrated to California. I, too, had been in that glorious region. I had seen the goodly land that it had been my heart's desire to visit, and returned satisfied.

"*Come on here, and settle down,*" cried Jack, out of the fulness of his quill pen. "*Come, and feast on bananas all the year round. I'll heap you up strawberries, luscious strawberries in pyramids, the top one, three bites to an eating. Lina will make you a salad out of humming-birds' thighs — I mean the sort of humming-bird that* HOPS. *You shall have cream as yellow as California gold, and sleep in a hammock as fine as gauze.*

"*Lina looks over* **my shoulder, and says** *she longs* **to see that** *little wife* **of yours.** *Her picture is mounted in a frame of mistletoe-berries, and stands on the table* **in** *our backwoods parlor.* **She** *looks like Elsa* **to a** *wonderful degree, but more like my Lina,—whose cough is better, thank you.* ·

"**By** *the way, Charlie, I've turned artist.* **My** *easel is made out* **of** *two youthful saplings, and my* **canvas is the bark** *of a curious tree that grows a* **few** *miles from* **here.** *But, upon my word, I should be afraid to show my picture;* **for** *I've copied the reds and yellows faithfully, and still they're not as red as the reds, or yellow as the yellows, of* **our** *Western skies; and* **I** *wouldn't blame the Eastern man who said to me what you said to the famous painter on one memorable occasion. Of course there's no use of putting our paper houses on canvas: we* **are** *only waiting for a good-sized earthquake to* **tumble them over,** *when I suppose we shall build them in a more substantial fashion.*

"*Our little familiar spirit, or sprite, young Elsa, is my attendant in my ground-floor atelier.* **She is** *just old enough to poison herself, and* **I'm** *afraid she will do it yet. Her mother dipped her yester-* **day** *out of a great tub of soft soap, remarking*

casually that it was the child's first lye. I told
her that was a good one, upon which she looked puz-
zled for a second, and then said, Oh! and laughed.
You would laugh, too, if you could see the youngster,
after a close examination of my pictures, with a ver-
milion nose, green eyebrows, and a forehead painted
like an Indian on the war-path. Genius, indeed!
Why that child has more genius for getting into
scrapes than any two men you can mention in the
whole circle of your acquaintance. And she's the
roundest specimen of the square Californian baby
that I ever saw. As soon as we can hire her to be
still for two consecutive seconds, after some artist
has settled down here, you shall have her picture.

" Now, remember that we are looking for you, and
that we can't take No for an answer; and come on."

I put down Jack's letter in rare good humor.
God bless your sunny correspondents! who never
skim the cream even of their choicest thoughts for
the delectation of strangers, and leave their friends
only the blue and watery milk of commonplaces.

"No, Jack," I said, mentally: "I sha'n't come
out to Santa Barbara this year, — next, perhaps."

And now for briefest glancing through the other
letters : trifles of note-queries, complaints ; here

and there a dart pointed with poison ; choice matter for future reference ;. pleas of poverty, "*Print,
or I die !*" complimentary, "*You look, Mr. Editor,
like a man who can comprehend,*" &c. ; flattering,
"*Dear Mr. Editor, when I saw your* **noble face ;**"
and so on to the end of the chapter.

Well, after all, it is a pleasant excitement to look
forward to, these letters from near and far. I have
seen "Mr. Speaker " at Washington fidget till he
got a sly glance at a letter or two or some packet
that lay quietly on his desk, and then he was ready
for business.

I was in an exceptionally happy mood : things
suited me without and within. I felt like a general surrounded by faithful aides : I called myself a
new Aladdin, with two or three old lamps to rub,
and an army of *genii* to wait upon me to whatever
wonders I might chance to wish for. Like bright
birds, new thoughts perched upon the branches of
my mind, and sang to me what I was to say Home
was delightful, my office cheerful, even the stand-
ard "devil" wore a shining face. How I should
write! I shut my eyes, trusting that fate would
keep bores, correspondents, friends, and acquaintances, at home for a good three hours ; and then I
went to work,

Two editorials : delightful ! the third was in progress. Thoughts breathed, words burned, at least to my self-satisfied comprehension ; and I was in the middle throes of an article on the war, when a gentle tap on the door, an opening sufficient to reveal bright eyes and a charming bonnet, and a flippant, " Do you mind my coming in ? "—unseated the greatest general living ; and caused my pen to weep a tear of ink to his fate, that blurred two of my most painstaking ideas.

" Certainly not, Mrs. Ellery : you are always welcome ; " and I forced a smile as our pretty, poetical contributor entered, her flounces trailing with a peculiarly stinging sound along the carpet.

Mrs. Ellery considered herself the fine wheat of womankind. She did write delightfully : there was no denying that. Her poems were bits of mosaic, put together with the most consummate skill : they were as marvellous in color as butterflies, flitted as brilliantly and swiftly before you, and were as soon forgotten, perhaps. She was well known to the publishers, — a breezy, smiling, golden-haired blonde, with a fine figure, exceptional jewels, and an audacious consciousness of her best points.

How a woman whose face indicated so little

real depth, being like a well and carefully painted
masterpiece in wax, with every feature in exactly
the right place, with shining teeth, and a mouth
just large enough to show them evenly when she
laughed, — could throw from her pen such pretty
and perfect lyrics and sonnets, has always been be=
yond my comprehension.   Her cool way of sailing
in, of forestalling all one's little mannerisms and
politenesses, of drawing her chair as close as possible to the editorial nose, of playing with the pens
and paper-knives, of catching at the drift of the
written pages, of chattering and holding one with
her eyes, of tossing her front hair into pretty
confusion, of making a telling *pose* — and then the
apparent unconsciousness of it all !

Her theme this morning was certainly a delightful one to an editor.   She was making an effort to
gather all her fugitive poems of the last five
mortal years.   They were scattered here and there
through five continuous piles, upon which, unless
the office-boy was a paragon among his fellows,
the dust lay thick ; and *would* I help her ?   Then
she grew eloquent upon the faults of publishers,
and in her earnestness actually buttonholed me
like any office bore.

I wore an old blue coat with brass buttons when on duty; and she seemed now, as she held the rusty effigy of some soldierly head between her dainty fingers, to be contemplating the hero of many fights, with her head now on this side, now on that, while she was so uncomfortably near me that I felt my color rise.

She possibly thought that I was admiring her, while I was mentally calling down thunderbolts upon her head. Several of the office men were privileged. Suppose old Sedges, the greatest cynic and sneerer since Diogenes, should take it into his head to come in for a bit of argument over some copy; or young Smythe, the wit of the composing *corps*, who didn't dare to say his soul was his own in the office, but made up for it by exceptional freedom of opinion outside, — and find this woman, whose poems I had openly admired, cheek by jowl with me as it were? The cold perspiration started from my joints; and, as if the fear had brought the judgment, the door did open just then, and admitted — that wife of mine.

Never judge a man by his looks when you pin a misdemeanor upon him; for, ten to one, the more innocent he really is, the more like a fool or a

guilty man he will act. To this day my cheeks
tingle as I **think of the** start with which **I sprang**
back as I **encountered Lissa's** surprised glance.
My **head** felt like drum-parchment drawn **to a** ten-
sion simply unbearable ; and my mouth involuntari-
ly screwed itself into position for a whistle, though
my leading desire was to smile a welcome. As
for Mrs. Ellery, she of course dropped the button,
and followed the direction of my eyes with a cool
nonchalance, evidently **thinking** that some rival
candidate for **poetic fame** had surprised our *tête-à-
tête*, and looking my little Lissa over with a quiet,
patronizing smile.

Though red to the throat, I managed **to get**
through with an introduction.

" My **wife,** Mrs. Ellery. — Lissa dear, this lady
is one of our poetical contributors."

" Dear **me, Mrs.** Harman ! **delighted, I'm** sure ; "
- **and** as Lissa, **in** her cool gray tints, and snowy
touches of lace, moved quietly forward, grace in
every movement, I somehow set my teeth hard as
the tinted glove of my correspondent touched the
innocent hand of my darling.

Not that I **knew any harm of Mrs.** Ellery ; but
her freedom of manner, and coquettishness of

action, were not the traits I desired in a friend of my wife ; and besides, I felt, rather than inferred, that Lissa was surprised and pained to find a beautiful woman, to use the popular and much-abused term, certainly a glib, showy, bright, and accomplished woman of the world, on such apparently confidential and intimate terms with her husband.

"I wanted to surprise you, dear," she said, as Mrs. Ellery withdrew, — and I am sure she was innocent of all intent to be sarcastic, — "so I came in without knocking."

"You are always privileged, you know," I answered with my sweetest smile : "I am so glad you are come!" She looked over my table, found a magazine which she opened with a reflective and somewhat pre-occupied air, put it aside, fingered a few papers, laid her parasol upon the table, looked out into the street, and said with a very conscious effort at unconsciousness, —

"Who was that lady, Charlie?"

"A Mrs. Ellery, my dear ; a correspondent of 'The Regulator,' and, in her way, a poet. You remember I showed you some of her little efforts ;" and I named two or three.

"Oh, yes! you read them to me : she is very

beautiful, is she not? Beautiful, and a poet! how nice for both to be!" A little pause: "Does she come here often?"

"As often as she has a poem to publish, or a favor to ask," I replied gravely. Long silence, and then a little sigh. I felt foolish, and tried to change the subject.

"Is it very hard, I wonder, to write poetry?" she asked at length, with a furtive glance at me.

"Not if one is born a poet," I made answer, looking longingly at my blurred manuscript.

"Am I in the way? yes, I must be," she said, in her quick, sharp tones when excited or angry, and rose.

"My dear, you are not in the least in the way: the other lady was," I added; and again that uncomfortable flush burned my cheeks.

"Ah! she who is so beautiful, and who writes so sweet poems, and who comes to my husband's office, and sits so near to him, nearer than *I* do;" and she pulled the chair which Mrs. Ellery had occupied, petulantly away.

"'Lissa!" I exclaimed, rising in consternation.

"Ah! don't say nothing to me: I am angry not — I have only a hurt heart. I cannot stay with dry eyes, — I cannot."

I tried to take her in my arms, but she burst
from me, as copy was called for ; and, to preserve
my dignity in the eyes of our chief compositor, I
coldly said, "Good-morning," and distributed copy
as she left the room.

Here was a serious dilemma.

That wife of mine! was she unmistakably
jealous ?

Chapter Eleven.

ATER in the afternoon Conrad came in. It was a rare thing to receive visits from him, except when, once in six months or so, he came to correct reports of his lectures before the college students and the faculty. I was not busy : indeed, I was reflecting whether I should not go home and have an explanation with my foolish little wife. But Conrad's coming changed my intention ; for really the interview was not a pleasant one to look forward to. A dozen times I had wished Mrs. Ellery at the antipodes. Why had she come, with her selfish instincts, to make trouble between two happy people ?

Conrad looked somewhat faded and careworn. In fact, he had not seemed quite like himself since the advent of that baby. For some moments he talked of electricity, on which he was preparing

an article for the paper. Then he fell into a
reverie; and the pallor of his face looked startling
with those large, luminous eyes gazing into va-
cancy.

"When do you lecture again, Conrad?" I asked
him, to break the spell of silence.

"Once perhaps, perhaps twice, before I leave
the college," was his answer.

"Leave the college! what are you thinking of,
man? You never would be so foolish."

"It is not as foolish as you think, perhaps,"
he murmured, with the old dreamy smile.

"But you are making your mark here: you
certainly have a fine career before you."

"Ay! I send up my fancies, and they come
down rainbows, I grant you; but they are only
bubbles. They dance and float, and then somebody gives them a pin-prick, and, *presto!* they are
less than the air, after all."

"But the college men are all your friends."

"So, so;" and he shrugged his shoulders.

"And your German class is very successful."

He changed color.

"Ah, that German class! I would like to
give that German class up," he exclaimed with
energy.

"Come, come, Conrad, out with it: you are in love."

He looked at me with a smile that was touching, because the corners of his mouth trembled.

"What is there in a face, an eye, a look, a trick of the muscles perhaps, that chains, entrances, makes a fool of a man? I never meant to, never in the world. You understand me: I was wedded to my classes, my ologies, my flute. So help me Heaven, I never meant to marry — and small chance if I do," he added, leaning over my desk in meditative mood.

"Miss Walters is a very sweet girl," I said, "something quite out of the common way; as exceptional in her individuality as my little Lissa."

"But Lissa had no father," he said in a bitter sort of tone.

"Ah! then you mean to say dean Walters is not favorable."

He shook his head.

"He is not the same man: that is all; and I don't understand what has changed him. Formerly he was cordial; he grasped my hand with a heartiness. But now he stands aloof, and it grows worse. He has, you know, a stern countenance;

but at times he is something awful of late, and I find it impossible to get near him."

"And the daughter?" I queried.

"Heaven knows! There is a change. I can scarcely define it: only, like a solid rock in my path, I know it is there. We Germans are psychological barometers."

"You Germans are a very imaginative and thin-skinned people," I said.

"Ah! after all, Germany is the only place," he said with quick enthusiasm. "There I have my home, my little garden, my peace."

"But you won't go and leave Lissa," I said, alarmed at I scarcely saw what in his manner.

"I hardly know yet, — I cannot tell. I shall finish the quarter of my German class, meet all my present engagements, then I shall see, — I shall see," he added meditatively.

"And poor Jo had such high hopes of becoming a German scholar!"

He looked at me as if he would look me through.

"Your sister will never make a German scholar," he said, as if against his will.

"And pray, why not?"

"She has not the metal, — not the continuing

faculty," he said, his eyes falling, and a little color tinging his cheeks. "She is not learning for a purpose, I think; only for the entertainment."

"Jo is a good, earnest girl."

"Very good, — very earnest;" and his eyes searched my face again. He seemed to hesitate as if some counter-force impelled him. "A good, earnest house-woman," he added, "such as German men like; such as make good wives and mothers."

"And how with Miss Walters?" I asked. "She is not your German type, is she?"

"Love makes all types one," he answered; "but she is too *spirituelle* for the German idea, — only the Americanized German would love her passionately. But I fear, nay, I know, she is not for me; and I would die for her."

He said this in a smothered voice, and then looked startled that he had spoken his feelings so strongly.

"Let us go home," he said, rising; and we walked together.

I did not see Lissa till we sat down to dinner. There was a perceptible change in her manner; and I noticed, when she helped me to meat, a small round spot on her little finger, that looked like ink.

Dinner over, she followed Conrad from the room, glancing back only when she reached the door to say, —

"I am going to have one of my old evenings with Conrad."

"Lissa!" I called. She paused for a moment, and then was going on.

"Lissa," I said softly, "you have forgotten something."

"You do not care so much for my kisses now," she said sorrowfully.

I held my arms open wide.

Very quietly and very slowly she came back.

"Do you know, little wife, that you are all the world to me?" I asked, as she was gathered in their fold. There was no answer.

"Are you going to leave me alone with my paper all the evening? Between Conrad and that baby, I feel like a sort of neglected pilgrim — sojourner in my own house."

"I — have some work to do," she said, disengaging herself.

"Cannot it be done when I am away? The duties of my office require so much of my time, and I am here but a few hours out of the twenty-four."

"Ah, your office!" she said, drawing back. "The duties there are *very* pleasant — if I may judge."

She made a demure courtesy, and was edging away from me, and I after her, determined to set myself right with regard to Mrs. Ellery, when the door opened, and Miss Walters's smiling presence surprised us both.

"I was going out with papa, and it came on to rain hard just at your door; so, as papa could not break his engagement, he said I might stay the evening with you, and he would call for me on his return."

"You came at an opportune time," I said; "for we were getting so tired of each other, that Lissa threatened to spend the evening with the professor."

"I've a great mind so to do now," said Lissa, laughing, "and carry Miss Walters up with me. She has never seen Conrad's den." All this time my little wife was divesting Miss Walters of her light summer wraps, and cooing over her. Can I give you an idea of this bright, lissome, dainty Nellie Walters? the hopeless desire of the college boys, who looked and sighed from a distance; the pet and darling of the lonely, learned dean; the love and delight of our noble Conrad? She was one girl of a thousand, — Lissa's counterpart in height and complexion, yet a complete contrast in manner and in temperament.

Her face held the calm and transparency of a clear flame unruffled by any atmosphere. Her greatest beauty was the exceptionally perfect contour of her head, which she never dressed in mountainous ridges of hair, but drawn well back and low, made a shapely curve near the nape of the neck out of her abundant tresses, as the Grecians did hundreds of years ago. Every thing she said and did bore the impress of strong vitality. There was the ring of energy in some of her low tones, though her voice had that peculiar quality of change which some call broken notes, yet if they were, were broken into exceedingly rich fragments of musical sound.

She looked the impersonation, as she stood there, of beauty, health, and intelligence.

Chapter Twelve.

RESENTLY Jo came in with the baby. The little one's name **was** Daisy, and she had become an institution. I think Lissa must have bent all the forces **of** her intellect to the adornment of the small princess, for her toilets were miracles of good taste.

Poor Jo had never appeared to advantage in Miss Nellie's presence; but, since the baby had created for itself a kingdom, she shone in **it for** what **she was** worth, because of her entire forgetfulness of self.

I believe, of all the household, she loved the little waif most tenderly. She certainly gave the most time and attention to its wants. I think my wife was prouder of the combination of baby beauty and French nurse, and loved to show them **off** together.

Miss Walters at first looked coldly upon the .

young Arab: at its entrance, I thought she changed color; but after a time she melted under its influence, and did her best to make it cry, by cuddling it and kissing it with undue but womanly vehemence. Then it was consigned to the nurse, and Jo marched after it to superintend the usual evening ablutions and arrangements.

Then Lissa disappeared, and after some time came down followed by Conrad in his best blue eye-glasses and his best black suit. There was an electric light in his face, giving it a splendor that all the riches of his scientific lore failed to impart. She whom he loved was there; and I sat apart, and watched the electric currents passing back and forth, gathering and giving and sparkling by turns, till the place became a paradise, and Conrad and Nellie Walters its Adam and Eve.

I shall never forget that evening, neither will Conrad. Our little room, pleasant in itself, seemed the receptacle of wit, cheerful fancies, and merry laughter. Conrad played the flute. Miss Walters had never heard him play before, and praised him with her sweet vermilion lips, till I knew his very heart ached with rapture.

And, when he talked, no wonder she hung upon

his words; for he had **the faculty** of language-painting in an unusual degree, and hung one picture after another before the eye, till silence was an absolute need, in which **to** admire the rich coloring and skilful grouping of these invisible but none the less real works of art.

As **I** said, I sat and watched. Did Miss Walters love him? She had been his pupil now for more **than** a year, with the twelve or fourteen rather ordinary girls **who** conned and repeated the German verbs with the precision of parrots; and it was her quick appreciation of the strength and beauty of the language, that first drew his interest like **a** magnet to her exceptional qualities of mind and person.

Lissa hovered about her, turning the music for her brother, — the proud Lissa! who took fire from the torch of his enthusiasm, and looked, while the clear and tender notes rolled heavenward, like a lesser St. Cecilia. And between the two passed lingering glances; one soliciting, the other giving, such sympathy as appertains between congenial natures; Lissa doing some unconscious wooing for **the** brother **she** was so proud and fond of. And occasionally Nellie Walters let her eyes rest upon.

the glowing face of Conrad. I who am somewhat
skilled in the telegraphy of — what shall I call it?
affinity? the word has been so outrageously abused
that I almost shrink from its use — felt that those
two creatures were so subtly kindred, the balance
of excess and lack of certain qualities being so
finely poised, that each would gain by the other in
what was needed in character or what to be pruned
away, that it was clear Providence had a hand in
their mating. But would Conrad, with his fine
sense of personal honor, be willing to fight for her
against the odds of parental injustice or prejudice?

Just then the sweetest melody of all ended, and
Nellie dropped her handkerchief, a catastrophe
that led to the broadest, brightest, most heavenly
conviction, that it falls to the lot of man to receive.
Conrad bent with supple spring to lift the bit of
lace and cambric from the floor. Nellie had already
stooped forward, and in lifting her head encountered whatever God and nature at that moment
gave his eyes the grace to say. And at that her
own eyes kindled; the heart of all rose-land
burned in her cheeks; her hand trembled as it
touched his. A pæan sounded, I am sure, from his
triumphant spirit at that moment, even to heaven.

She loved him !

To her, love meant for now and for ever.

Lissa had seen. She edged her way round **to** me after a time, with the coyness of a youthful bride ; and some way her hand got in mine, and **I** felt, that, for the present, Mrs. Ellery and her poetry were consigned to oblivion.

It was not the time exactly for the dean to step **in,** with his judicial aspect, and his love-memories twenty years away ; but he did. He caught sight of the flute : he glanced dubiously at Conrad, who with folded arms was trying, I suppose, to hold his heart-leaps down. Then he edged himself between the twain, put on his daughter's wraps so clumsily that any one might have seen it was an unusual duty ; and, taking Miss Walters by the arm like **a bear trying to do** the honors after the most amiable **fashion; he led her** from the house.

" You'll not pack your trunks to-night, I fancy," I found an opportunity to whisper as he unscrewed his flute.

" I sha'n't go to Germany without — Lissa," he retorted, laughing. After that, peace and harmony prevailed; only some way that wife of mine gave me now and then secret misgivings. Was it Lissa who met me with abstracted glances, who seemed to be always looking at her hands, through the walls, over the teapot, at nothing ; who smiled in the wrong place, and answered that she didn't know what you were saying, after you had explained to her in the most glowing language the latest invention in apple-parers, or the newest patent in coffeepots ?

"My dear, what were you saying ?" she asked one day when I sedulously depicted my labors in finding something for which she had expressed a wish.

For answer I held a jewel-box exactly under her nose. She gave one delighted cry, and grasped it with both hands.

"They are just as lovely as they can be ! are they for me ?"

"Who should I get them for if not for you, *mignonne ?*"

"They are very much the same in pattern as Mrs. Ellery's," she said.

"How do you know about Mrs. Ellery's jewels ?" I asked. She was silent for a moment. The color flitted in her cheek. Then she looked up at me almost defiantly.

"She showed them to me."

"She showed them to you — when?"

"I had not meant to tell you," she made slow answer; "but — but I went there."

"You went to Mrs. Ellery's?"

"Yes, I did."

"You went to that down-town hotel?"

"What harm was there?"

"Without telling me that you were going?" I questioned in holy horror.

"Why should I do that? Do you tell me everywhere that you do go?"

Here was a poser; but I did not stop to consider, or to soften matters.

"You are a woman, I am a man: on matters of business I am supposed to go anywhere, everywhere; but you!"

"And, if I had matters of business, why should I not go anywhere, everywhere?"

Here was a small woman's-rights association growing under my very eyes.

"But, my dear, I am the business head of the house. You are to manage in doors, I out."

"You have no more business-head than I have," she ejaculated indignantly. "When Conrad travelled, and took me with him, *I* kept all the accounts, and paid all the moneys. Yes, I did, and he will tell you so. And do you suppose he could leave his books, and go and buy steaks and potatoes? Yes, and I did hire rooms, and pay for them."

Chapter Thirteen.

FELT **all my** pretensions to superiority oozing out at my fingers' ends ; but like **a** man, and a very ordinary sort of man **at** that, I determined to **hold my** ground.

Lissa had never before boasted of her accomplishments in the way of business. I never **knew** that she was an expert in culinary **purchases, a** book-keeper in a small but expeditious **way,** a person with experience in letting and sub-letting ; **in** fine, a whole bureau **of** expedients **and** experiments. **I had** more yet to learn.

" **But** about this going **to** call upon Mrs. Ellery : what in the world set you at it ? I thought you were not pleased with her."

" I was not, oh, no ! but I reasoned with myself. **I felt that she** must be in some **way a** very superior person. If you **knew** her, **and —and** liked **her** for her genius, you know, why should not I ?

I determined not to have prejudice which might do harm to an innocent lady ; and so — so I called."

" And you found her in ? "

" Oh, yes ! with two, three, four gentlemen, all *littérateurs* she said, and introduced me as your wife. Then they said things that made me very proud of you."

" The Bohemians ! " I muttered between my teeth.

" Lissa," I said firmly, " you must not go there again."

" Do you say I must not ? "

" Most imperatively. I forbid it."

She rose, growing pale, and actually growing tall, as the spirited face changed color.

" You shall not say ' I forbid,' to me," she articulated with provoking distinctness. " Even when I was that small," holding her hand at some distance from the floor, " Conrad never said to me, ' I forbid.' If I like Mrs. Ellery, and she is kind to me, and — and I am satisfied with what she does for me, why should I not call upon her, and have her come here ? "

In a sudden frenzy of unreasonableness, I said, " She shall not come here : it is against my wishes

and my commands," I asserted, losing my temper
for the first time.

"She shall come here," was the firm retort.

Here was open rebellion. One of us, I foolishly
said to myself, must be master in this matter; and
clearly the right was on my side. Lissa's will was
a small battery. I felt its power, and for the first
time acknowledged that I had looked upon her too
much in the light of an indulgent father. She
was a child to be petted, encouraged, and guided,
heretofore; now I waked up to the fact that she
was a force in my life, and the only question was,
had I strength enough to oppose and control her?
If we were not to work together, there was an end
to our happiness. I should have scorned the
thought of conquering her, of merging her individuality with mine, of making her even a willing
slave to my whims and humors. Suddenly some
good angel lifting his shining wings must have
poised himself on my shoulder, directly under my
right ear; for I distinctly heard the words, "Yield
if you would conquer."

"Very well, Lissa," I said quietly. "Since you
are determined to make a friend of this woman,
you may if you will. I shall no longer oppose
you."

She looked at me out of those steady eyes of hers ; and I saw the little demon of self-will poising himself for flight.

"Mrs. Ellery may come here?"

"Certainly." ·

"And I may go there?"

"Yes."

"But it — it will not please you?" she said, in a lower voice.

"I cannot say that it will, and be honest."

"Will you give me your reasons?"

Surely: why had I not thought of that before?

"Because, you know, she can come to see *you*," she added naïvely.

"Why — y-es. An editorial office is a public place. A great many people come there I should not care for you to know."

"Ladies?"

"Well, no, not many ladies but are quite worthy of your friendship; but the most of them are poor, hard-working contributors, and cannot afford the time to make acquaintances or to visit. Mrs. Ellery may be one of the noblest women in the world, for all I know; but she is not a careful woman. Her talk is loud and slangy; she allows

dangerous intimacies, wears too many jewels, enter-
tains too many gentlemen ; and, worse than all, she
has adopted socialistic theories, and does not believe in the sacredness of the marriage-bond as we
do, sweet wife of mine."

"Ah, now you make me to see !" she said, bringing her hands lightly together.   "You treat me as
an equal : you appeal to my reason, my pride, my
religion.   That is good and right; and now it is
very proper for me to obey you."

"Is that the right word, little woman ?   I know
sundry of our acquaintances who would cavil at it
mightily."

"Yes, perhaps, but it troubles not me.   I
obeyed Conrad always, though not of fear; and
it is your wish for me to do so, or to do not so,
why should I not obey it ?   It is my wish, with
proper reasons, that you do not so, or so, why
should you not obey?   Are you too proud because you are a man ?   Then will I be too proud
because I am a woman."

"My small teacher of equality," I said, "you
have put the shoe on the other foot with admirable
skill, and I am happy to tell you it fits.   Hence-
forth I am yours to command."

My compensation came in due course of time.

Not many days after, I went home at noon, not feeling very well; and, on lying down, hung my watch on a hook in the wardrobe. Being obliged to return to the office at a later hour, I neglected to re-instate my watch in its fob.

As I walked hurriedly down the street I met an old friend just returned from Europe.

"Charlie Harman! as my name is Paul!" he exclaimed, giving me a hearty hand-grasp.

I remembered subsequently, that, as I talked with him after the manner of auld acquaintance-ship, a young fellow with sandy hair and an equiline nose, on whose protuberant arch lay a rather seedy hat that hid his eyes, stood quietly leaning against a lamp-post within a foot of where we were; but I thought nothing of it then.

"And where are you now? at the same old office?" asked Paul.

"Yes, office of 'The Regulator;'" and in taking my cards out of my pocket I must have let one of them slip into the gutter.

"What's the time?" queried Bennington when he recollected that time and tide wait for no man.

"My watch is set by a British clock."

I felt in my pocket.

"I declare! I've not done such a thing for a dozen years," said I.

"What's that?"

"Left my watch hanging up in the wardrobe;" and with a few more last words we parted.

I staid at the office only long enough to make a scratch or two on the proof, which was always a perfect kaleidoscope of pen-and-ink sketches, owing to my writing an "awful hand," the terror of compositors, and the despair of my wife, who prided herself on her legible chirography.

Ensconced on the dining-room sofa, far away from all noise save the pleasant bustle of preparation for tea, I was soon lost in pleasant reflections. At last a thought occurred to me. Lissa came in looking as dainty as a bird in a brown suit. She was approaching me joyously.

"First a kiss and then a favor," I said, laughing.

"Of course. When you are very loving I always wonder what you are going to ask me."

"Will you run up stairs, and bring me down my watch?"

She stood there like one petrified.

"Your watch!" she exclaimed.

" Yes, dear, my watch : I left it in the ward-robe."

Her face changed : a scale of gradations passed over it, till with open mouth and scared eyes she could only repeat again, —

" Your watch ! "

" Lissa, dear, what is the meaning of this ? " I asked. " Is it too much trouble ? because, though I am not well, I will go."

I rose, but she held me down.

" O Charlie ! what shall I do ? " and she burst into tears.

I was now thoroughly alarmed.

" My dear, if any thing has happened to it, if you let it fall, if the crystal is broken, I will bear it with the utmost fortitude, and forgive you with the greatest magnanimity."

" But — but — I sent it to you."

" You sent it to me ! Heavens and earth ! When ? "

" Not quite half an hour after you had left the house.

" My dear, what superhuman prescience told you that I wanted my watch in exactly thirty minutes ? for it was then — or about ten minutes

before that, **to** speak with precision —that I dis-
covered I had left **it**."

"It was no prescience : it was a **man**."

"He couldn't have stolen it, **because you sent it
to** me ; but why in the name of the Ganges **did
you do that?** It cost me five hundred dollars,
including chain and charms; a stem-winder, and
regulated the sun to the fiftieth part of **a second**."

"But didn't you send for it ?"

"**Never!**"

"By a man with yellowish hair and blue eyes,
who said he worked in the office ?"

"Never : there isn't a yellow hair in the whole
office."

"**O** Charlie! then I have lost you your watch,"
and Lissa caught hold of the sofa.

"**I give you** leave to lose a thousand watches,
but not to faint away over it," I said, as, I offered
her a cup of cold water. "Come, tell me all about
it. Somebody has imposed upon you ; but maybe
we can get a clew to the rascal, and find the
watch."

"**Stop : you** sent your card," she said, and took
from her pocket my card, slightly soiled. I looked
it over : it had evidently been in the gutter. On
the back was something **in my handwriting**.

"My dear, if you had only *read* this !" I said.

"Well, what if I had?" said Lissa, restraining her tears with difficulty. "What is it?"

I read, —

"Tell Bob to bring buttermilk ; buy watch-key ; mend office-window immediately."

She laughed through her tears.

"It's an old memorandum, made weeks ago ; and the scamp, not being able to read himself, presumed upon your ignorance."

"But, my dear Charlie, I didn't try to read it : I never do. It all looks like chickens' legs to me. I saw something that seemed like 'bring,' and 'watch,' and 'office ;' and, oh, dear! I thought to be sure it was all right, especially when he gave your name and number. Charlie, dear, why don't you try to write so that one might be able to spell it out?"

"I don't know," said I musingly, "why people should find fault with my handwriting: it's plain enough to me. But I'm sure of one thing: I'm a watch and chain out."

"And all through me," said Lissa.

"If a man should come to you again, my dear, for my best coat, you will please follow the Scrip-

ture injunction, and give him my cloak also:
though, on second thought, I haven't any cloak;
but you might throw in a hat."

"Charlie, I'm so sorry!" sobbed Lissa. "If you'll
wait long enough, I'll make up the loss: I will,
really. I'll earn it."

"I can't afford to wait for a watch 'till my locks
are like the snaw,' Mrs. Anderson," said I, assum-
ing a light manner. "The best way will be to lose
no time in eating supper; and then Conrad and I
will make the rounds, and put detectives on the
track of that keen eavesdropper, who, I remember
now, stood near enough to hear all we said. If you
had only read the card!"

"But that was impossible," said Lissa: "I can't
make it out."

"So the compositors say; but they do," was my
reply.

Chapter Fourteen.

CONRAD and I were busy with detectives till nearly eleven o'clock. It was almost twelve before we finished our business, and turned our tired feet homeward. The night was very dark. Locked arm in arm, we walked silently, till at last Conrad broke the silence in a low voice, —

"There's a woman following us."

"Yes; I noticed it a square or two back: she keeps exactly behind us, poor soul!"

"It is very strange, she comes so close, and never speaks," said Conrad. "It may be some miserable creature who is dying of hunger. I always think that."

"Nonsense! compose your nerves, my good Conrad. You are not as familiar with these city streets as I am. You wouldn't care to speak to the kind of woman who goes roaming at this hour of the night."

" Still, even if she is unfortunate, a kind word, to learn if she is suffering ! She haunts me like a spirit," persisted Conrad.

" **If** you are determined to see for yourself, **see**," I said doggedly ; and we stopped. The thing in human form, whatever **it was**, stopped also, and, **just** discernible in the dim light of a corner **street**-lamp, looked weird to the last degree, as its loose drapery fell lightly about it, and it seemed to hover **just over the pavement.**

" Come, **come!** whatever it is, it's apparently afraid of us," **I said** ; and, gracious Heaven ! somebody exclaimed, " Charlie !"

Again the voice, so much louder than **the last** cry that I could hear it tremble.

" Great Heaven, it's Lissa !" I said, and called her. She came **flying** towards me, and fell into my arms **with a** half-hysterical scream.

" **I** hoped **it was you.** O Charlie ! I'm almost **dead** with fright."

" In the name of the Vedas of India, Lissa Harman, what **are** you doing out here in the dead of night ?" I asked.

" Don't **scold, Charlie.** I got lost, and no soul **in** sight; **and** the dark, and the **strange look** of the streets, made my heart beat till I thought I should fall. Then I saw you two, and I thought of Charlie and Conrad ; and I began to follow you, though I was afraid of you. When you stopped and looked back, I had like to run away ; but something told me to call you, and, if it was you, you would speak."

"But will you please explain why you are out at this unseemly hour ?" I asked impatiently.

"Why, the baby "—

"Condemn that baby," I groaned.

"Now, Charlie ! "

" Your pardon, Mrs. Harman : I interrupted you ; a thing that you are never guilty of — if you will allow me to tell a polite lie."

"Charlie, you are angry, and you won't let me explain ; but I will. The baby was taken in spasms, then, and we sent for the doctor next door."

"Well ?"

"He staid till poor little Daisy was better, then wrote a prescription."

"Of course : do you know he will charge five dollars for that ?"

"Charlie, are you mean ?"

"Well, I have just lost five hundred dollars, my dear," I said, as mildly as I could. "And now to find you running the streets on account of that little beggar!"

She loosened her arm from mine, and deliberately walked round to the professor.

"Lissa," said I, stung by my own injustice, "if you'll come back I'll ask your pardon."

"No; ask no pardon: I will come without that, if you are sorry; but you must listen, for indeed I cannot see Daisy die before my eyes for the want of a little medicine," she said falteringly. "Well, it was then half-past ten. The doctor told us she must have the powders immediately, or there might be a return of the illness. I thought you would soon come in, but you did not. At quarter to eleven I begged the nurse to go: she would not stir; she had never been out so late, she said, and I could not hire her. At eleven I could wait no longer: I remembered having seen drug-shops at different corners, but did not know exactly where to go. Disguising myself in my waterproof, I came out. Oh, it was so dark! so silent! not a step all down the long street. I had never, in all my life, been out in the dark alone."

"My brave little wife," I whispered, squeezing her arm.

"Not a bit: I felt like a weak coward; but I braced up the courage, and I went on, square after square, and still no shops of the kind; oh, for so long a distance! A poor drunken sailor came along; but he only stood still for a moment, as well as he could for reeling, and said, in German, —

"'God bless the woman!'

"O Charlie! hearing that dear language! if he had only been sober, I should have asked him to take care of me. I went on till I came to such a queer little corner drug-shop, with such an old, queer man behind the counter, all hair and teeth, for all the world like our old white dog Wolf, at home in Germany.

"He looked at me, and at the paper, and then at me again, and said something about up-town doctors, and they didn't generally send prescriptions to him: so you see how far I had gone. Not long after I left him, I seemed to have got bewildered, turned round, you know: the streets looked strange. Where should I go, and who should I speak to? O Charlie, how I did long for you! just as if I were in a foreign land, and you thousands of miles away.

When the terror had hold of me that I did not know which way to go, of all the streets I met, I stood still for a moment, and I thought of our God who sees us in all our troubles, and I told him how I wanted Charlie; and that minute you came in sight ; but I didn't quite believe, — it is always so, you know,—and so I followed you two, fearing and hoping, till I got the strength to speak ; and, O Charlie ! it's *so* good to be here ! "

Now, find me a narrative more simple than that, more commonplace if you will ; and yet I declare to you that the tears were running over my cheeks before I knew it.

"Lissa," said I, "you're a heroine ! I'm proud of you ; and — and — God bless the baby ! "

As for the professor, who had been silent, I saw he couldn't bear the light of the hall-lamp, though it was very low ; and so a woman with her little story had set two men to crying.

I am happy to add, as a pleasurable ending to this chapter, that my watch was traced to a pawn-broker's shop, and restored to me.

Chapter Fifteen.

AMONG my letters the day following, was one from a lady correspondent, a brilliant, gossipy writer, who kept us informed as to the comings and goings of society people, and who could write about the embroidery upon a French flounce with as much enthusiasm as your art-student when revelling in the description of one of Turner's best pictures.

While reading it, I was struck with her reference to a visit she had recently made.

"Finding myself in H—— the other day," she said, "and having some three or four hours on my hands, it struck me that I might employ my leisure in exploring the neighborhood.

"To the right on a grandly rising eminence, stood an imposing edifice of gray stone, which I found upon inquiry was a hospital for the insane. Curiosity, and I trust, profound pity for such unfor-

tunates, led me to apply for admission.   I was
told that it was not the day for public inspection ;
but when I showed them the magic name of 'The
Regulator,' and explained that I wrote (for very
small pay, you know) for its columns, the sealed
doors opened, and I entered.

"Every thing seemed to be in apple-pie order,
notwithstanding it was not a show day ; and two or
three of the nurses, barring a certain disagreeable
firmness about the mouth, impressed me favorably.
The doctor, a portly Sir Chesterfield sort of man,
with a head like a lion, narrow shoulders, and a
terrible eye which I fear would drive me insane
if I had too much of it, explained all the workings
of the institution, which I will not now trouble
you with.

"One of the patients was a slender, hectic
woman, who ceased her rocking as I came near,
and, rushing towards me with clasped hands, cried
piteously, —

"'Have you seen my baby ?'

"'That is her cry, madam, morning and night,'
said the doctor.

"'Is the child dead?' I asked.

"'We fear so," he replied carefully, and in an

aside. 'Undoubtedly it perished by her hands; but she was not responsible, having lost her mind before its birth. It was born here.'

"What a pitiful story! Do you follow it? Born in a madhouse! its inheritance insanity!

"Her mind was wrecked by the sudden death of her husband. They were riding side by side, when the horse took fright, and threw them both out. He was instantly killed before her eyes, while she was uninjured. She never smiled afterward; grew melancholy, and at last raving mad. After the birth of the child, her insanity took a milder form; but she seemed to fear visitors wanted to take her babe, and resorted to the most novel methods to hide it. Sometimes the poor soul would secrete it in the grounds, in curious corners and out-houses, but always with an eye to its safety. At last one day in June, she made her escape; and when found the child was not with her. At first she said she had hidden it where no one could find it, then that she had given it away; and at last she mourned for it incessantly. The woods were searched and the rivers dragged as far as practicable, but no trace was ever found of the child. Undoubtedly she made way with the poor little soul: if not, God help it!"

Judge if I was not surprised, gratified, startled, enlightened. The place was less than a mile from the little side station where Conrad had stopped on that eventful day; the time June; the circumstances coincident.

I took up the letter again.

"Since then," continued my fair correspondent, "the mother fancies that they have found the child, and are keeping it from her. To every visitor she puts the same melancholy query, —

"'Have you seen my baby?'

"Day after day she waylays the attendants and even the doctor himself, pitifully entreating them to give up the child, and offering fabulous sums for its restoration. They answer her kindly, it is to be hoped, for the poor soul is drawing very near the grave. The doctor thinks she cannot last many weeks. She is a slight, sweet-looking woman; but her face is so stamped with unchanging sadness, that one cannot forget it. It has followed me for days and days."

I hurried home with the letter to Lissa. She read it through quietly and with a very grave face.

"The baby must go to its mother," said Lissa.

"But how do we know that she is its mother?"

"Why, of course it is: don't you see? I'm as sure of it as if I had been on the spot, and witnessed the whole transaction."

"You have been just as sure of other things," I said, "and yet been mistaken."

"Oh, yes! I know that: I'm not a bit wise; I never shall be, I suppose."

"And I don't want you to be, not at least till I cut my own wisdom teeth," I made reply. "We are only grown children at the best, but I must say you are the most delightful specimen I ever encountered."

"You forget Elsa," she said reprovingly.

"No; for in you I have my Elsa reduplicated. I somehow love you both in one. Does that trouble you?"

"On the contrary, it charms me. If I were looking down from where she is, and you disparaged *me* in the slightest degree, I would go seek another love in heaven; but if you talked of me as you do of your Elsa, I should want to clasp you both in my arms and never lose you."

"Well, that is rather vague as to personality and identity," was my reply; "but we'll put it to the account of the German tongue."

"I never can be jealous of the dead," she said softly and musingly, "because if I should die"—

I caught her in my arms, and smothered the unwelcome words down upon her lips with kisses.

"You are not going to die: you are going to live to torment me till my gray hairs are uncountable; get me into scrapes innumerable, laugh me out of my absurdities, and cry me into them again. You are a witch-woman, Lissa; you are a German Lorelei without her wickedness; I think you must have been the maiden of the Drachenfels some hundreds of years ago, who subdued even the dragon. Well, I won't be foolish any more. But how about the baby?"

"I shall take it there immediately."

"And am I to have nothing to say about it?"

"What do men know about such matters?"

"I humbly bow to your superior knowledge; but it strikes me, that as I have a little business in that vicinity, it would not be amiss to stop at the hospital, and learn whether the state of the woman is such that it would be advisable to carry the child there."

"Y-es, maybe it would; perhaps you are right," she assented a little reluctantly.

Accordingly, after a short consultation with the professor, I ran down to H. The result was a telegraph line to Lissa :—

" Woman is dead ; was buried yesterday."

I saw Perkins, the little oil-man, with a rag in one hand and a lamp in the other; I looked out of the narrow windows to the long stretches of woods on either side, at the two shining rails that faded into indistinctness ; I thought of the poor, mindless mother, dying with her longing unsatis-fied ; and my heart went out to the orphan waif as it never had gone before.

Chapter Sixteen.

"YOU'LL send the piano, dear: mind you don't forget."

"I'll send the piano: I won't forget. You want a *grand*, don't you?"

"Of course; one of the best; and two stools, please, for the duets."

"All right; stools for the duets. They'll be here by three at the latest, if I live long enough to order them."

"Now, Charlie, you are very forgetful."

"I know it, but this is an important commission. All the forces of my intellect have been brought to bear upon the proper exercise of the functions of memory. I shall *not* forget. *Au revoir*."

I did not forget. There were rival music stores, Dexter's and Woufert's. Woufert advertised in "The Regulator," Dexter did not: consequently I felt myself in duty bound to patronize the little bald-headed German, Woufert.

We were to have a small, select company to listen to a new star in the musical world. Conrad had invited the college faculty, including the dean. The latter wrote a rather stiff little note, excusing himself and his daughter, which Conrad tore in pieces as soon as he read it.

Von Lewes was the name of our new musical celebrity. He had promised to take tea with us, in order to enjoy a *tête-à-tête* in German with my wife and the professor. I had invited several editors of city journals, ordered ice-cream *ad libitum*, and felt myself beating time to the anticipated harmony as I cheerfully hummed over my work.

Woufert offered me his best piano, — one that he said had been tested by experts, and the sale of which was now under consideration between two parties, one of whom, the Swedish consul, would be sure to buy.

The day passed happily away. Bores went by the door. Contributors wrote pleasantly. I was prepared to feel that the world was a harbor of rest for weary souls, as I took my way homeward. Suddenly, in fronting my house, I became aware of a scene of unusual and perplexing annoyance.

Two immense vans, each loaded with a grand piano of the largest calibre, blocked up the passage; and the drivers thereof were abusing each other in the purest idiomatic Irish, while six brawny men on either side were vociferating at the top of their lungs, — ordering, contradicting, jeering, and jesting, to the lively amusement of all the boys for a dozen streets round. Two hurdy-gurdy performers and a swarthy Italian, with hand-organ and monkey, had paused to listen and to laugh.

Here was a dilemma. I came upon the situation just as the two Milesian drivers were tearing off what fragments of coats covered their rags, each protesting that he would knock the other into smithereens. Respectable windows on each side of the street held their quota of respectable and shocked faces. Here and there a voice cried, "Police!"

"See here, men, what's all the trouble?" I asked.

Imagine the irate Irishmen, both talking in what was double Dutch to me, flourishing their whips, pulling their beards, jerking heads, hands, and elbows.

Just then, looking up at a square of window, I saw Lissa's face. Its lineaments were despairing to the last degree. Her rapid telegraphy summoned me within; but I felt that this ridiculous scene must be made an end of; for the street was nearly blocked up, as sundry drivers, with their vehicles, had also stopped to see what was going on. During this time, the two noble but wrathful sons of Erin never abated their shibboleth.

"Men," I said, "which of you comes from Woufert's?"

"It's mesilf, shure," cried the tallest, with a touch-me-if-you-dare leer at his rival.

"You're the one I want, then; and I'll give the other a dollar to back out. There's some mistake here."

"By the bones of St Patrick! I should say there was," repeated the discomfited Erinite, who had been so politely informed that he was not wanted, as he scratched his red head vigorously.

"Make quick work of it, boys. Here's your dollar; and I'll come round to Dexter's, and see that it's all right."

Woufert's man gave his rimless hat a spin, and fairly howled his ecstasy. The other, with more venomous words, and vindictive shakes of his head, than I can enumerate, backed out, to the consternation of all the boys, and the fright of **the** girls, who decamped forthwith.

· I had fairly taken in **the** situation, **when I met** Lissa in **the** small **reception-room.**

" Well, my dear, all Oak Street has been notified **that we** are **to** give a social *musicale.* **It** was a good advertisement."

"Charlie, it's too bad!" she said, with tears **in** her eyes.

" What is too bad ? "

" Why, every **thing. The** disgusting conduct of those two men ! Conrad **could** do nothing **with** them. And in the midst of it all, came your musical friend. He could **hardly get into the house.** What must he think ? "

" **I** suppose ·he simply wondered which was the best piano. But, Lissa ! "

She cowered a little, like a child sensible of its · error.

" Three o'clock came, and — and nothing else. I thought you **had** forgotten : Conrad thought so too."

" I hope, my dear, that some day you will see the grandeur and justice of trusting your husband," I said quietly and deliberately.

She was silent for a single moment.

"Conrad said you traded with Dexter," she murmured: "he gets all his music there."

"Who ordered it?"

"I did."

"And you paid down for it?"

"Yes, of course: ten dollars."

"Just exactly what I paid at Woufert's; but never mind, love, what is money? Does not the immortal Johnson say that money and time are the heaviest burdens of life? Let us not regret our twenty dollars, then. But perhaps you also ordered ice-cream and other sundries, for fear that I forgot."

"And if I did?"

"We'll sell it to-morrow, to defray expenses."

"I think you are the most hatefullest person that ever was living. Can't you see how sorry I am? Can it now be helped? Do you know what I felt with all the fuss going on, and the fighting, and the crowd, and the dread of seeing you come home, because I had done thoughtless?"

"Lissa, I am sorry."

"I don't care: you are always being sorry, and always being unjust. I should have married in my own country."

"Why, Lissa, you did marry in your own country — but you made a mistake in the man, eh? Come, honest."

"No!" very short.

"Your husband is a great tyrant, who wants his own way in every thing; an absurd creature who loves jokes better than his food, and scolds his wife where he only means to laugh at her, — that is, she thinks he scolds her. And then she don't have confidence in him; and as he's a great, good-natured fellow, she *will* boss him now and then."

"Never!" angrily: "I never did in mine life."

"Only a little, just a little, to give spice to the quiet of our existence."

"And *you* never make mistakes, never do outrageous things?"

"Yes, I do: I am going to do an outrageous thing to-morrow — see!"

"Oh, opera!" she cried, her eyes sparkling.

"Yes, and a box at that. Have you a pretty dress?"

"Charming! blue silk: I have worn it but once; and white cloak with the birds' down. O Charlie, how nice you are!"

"How about that German you should have married?"

"There never was a German half as good as you
— only Conrad."

"And you forgive me the ten dollars ?"

Her laugh rang out.

"O Charlie! you should have seen the fun. First
drove up one; and no sooner had he rung the
door, than up came the other. And then they
stood on the doorstep, talking to Tiddy; and Tiddy
threatened to throw hot water on them, and I came
down and begged them to wait a little. Then they
climbed to their seats, and presently began joking
each other, and grew angry, and the little boys
cheered. I can laugh at it now, because it seems
so ridiculous; but I could have cried, and then I
was so mortified to think it was all my doing. I
was so sure you had forgotten it when Mr. Dexter
said you had not been in at all. How did I know
about the other music-store ?"

Did ever man have a more charming wife ? She
could have had the half of my kingdom for the
asking.

Chapter Seventeen.

ALBANI sang that night in the opera "Sonnambula," which was a favorite of Lissa's. Like a white star set in blue, my little wife shone beside me; and I confess to being quite elated by the admiration she excited.

Perhaps it was a drawback to find Mrs. Ellery also an occupant of our box, in company with two young men about town, instead of her lawful husband. Lissa's greeting was constrained, but Mrs. Ellery never accepted a slight. She was more than ordinarily gracious to **my** wife : she devoted herself to me equally with her two cavaliers. It was in that quality of making herself agreeable to any number of gentlemen, and in such a way that each one felt himself flattered by her exclusive preference, that Mrs. Ellery excelled.

" What a powerful voice ! how deliciously **clear** and pure ! " she observed, leaning over Lissa, and shaking her rich laces with the effort. "Do you notice the middle register? You must let me write her up for you, will you? I so dote on Albani!"

"You have my permission, certainly," I said.

"What an atmosphere of poetry she must carry about with her perpetually!" she continued. "Do you know, she has set a dozen sonnets flying through my brain? 'Oh, spring-tide bloom!' is one which is slowly shaping into roundness and finish. Does your wife write? — Do *you* ever write poetry, Mrs. Harman? you look as if you did."

Lissa blushed, and her eyes appealed to me.

"I am sure she could, Mrs. Ellery, if she tried; but my wife's poetry is in her home-surroundings, and her husband reads it every day in the grace and comfort she creates."

"Very pretty, I'm sure. Your husband has not yet ceased to be your lover, Mrs. Harman," she said, laughing. "If we poor women could always be so appreciated! But ah! Albani is singing, *Ah, non credea!* What a shame that I should talk!"

After a time, and when there was a brief lull in the music, she leaned over again.

"There is a **very** pretty woman **who** constantly eyes you **through** her glass, **in** one **of the** opposite boxes," she said to me. I looked in the direction indicated, so did Lissa.

"She is pretty, indeed she is **very pretty**," said Lissa. "**Do you** know her?"

"**I do** not," was **my** reply.

"**You** should consider it a compliment : she **looks at no one** but **you**," continued Mrs. Ellery. "**I have been** watching her : **she** must be talking of **you, too, to** somebody **hidden by** the curtain."

In a few moments a **card was** handed **to me.** The name was one which **I** was not familiar with, but I stepped out of my box to meet **the gentle-** man who sent it.

"Will **you go** round **with me?**" he asked, "to see an old friend of yours?"

I could do **no** more than **excuse myself to** Lissa, **and in a** short time found **myself,** to my intense surprise, the occupant of **the** box opposite, indicated by Mrs. Ellery, and seated beside the lady who had used her opera-glasses **so** indefatigably **during the** evening.

If ever mortal man was **placed in a** dilemma, **I** was that night. I found the lady in question an old friend of my youth ; and, on closer inspection, her beauty was not so fresh as it looked across the house. If you have ever been caught between two rapid talkers who value nothing so highly as their own vocal powers, who question you, ply you with facts, go into long genealogical researches, and who, in fine, are never so happy as when talking of themselves, you will imagine the perplexity I was in. In vain I tried to excuse myself, hinted that I had left my wife alone : my tormentors had me by the button, and were determined to keep me.

I thought I saw a smile of fiendish satisfaction on Mrs. Ellery's face as one of the young men took my seat beside Lissa. And, was it possible? was that my wife laughing, talking to him, playing with her fan, her cheeks red, her eyes intense with light, her manner gracious ?

I saw Mrs. Ellery bend over and speak to Lissa, and Lissa answer back with unwonted freedom. Her manner I could tell was the outgrowth of some new emotion. Presently glasses were levelled towards her. People seemed but just finding out that there was a beauty, a new, fresh importation, the burning gold of whose hair under the lustres was not **to** be matched in all that great assembly.

It was not till near the close of the last act that **I** could free myself of my tormentors.

" Tell your charming wife that I shall do myself the honor of calling and making her acquaintance," laughed the lady; " but pray don't add the sentimental fact that you **were an** old **beau of mine.**"

" I don't think I shall, madam," was **my** mental answer, and hurrying away I entered my own box. There was no seat for me now except behind Lissa; and beyond a cold nod Lissa never recognized me. The young jackanapes beside her coolly kept **my** chair, completely ignoring me; and, unless Lissa had signified the wish, I had not **the nerve** just then to ask him to resign my place. So we **sat** there, — **I** sullen and **moody ;** Lissa gay by fits **and** starts, **talking much** to Mrs. Ellery, who pretended great confidences, but never once speaking **to** me till the entertainment was over.

" Well, have you enjoyed yourself ? " I asked, as I drew Lissa's cloak closer over her throat.

" Not **a** bit," she answered with **a** rapid gesture.

" If she hasn't, I know somebody who has," laughed Mrs. Ellery, who overheard us.

"If you mean me, madam," I said coldly, "I give you much credit for your penetration: if you mean the gentleman who came with you, I'm afraid he needs more brains to be capable of enjoying any thing besides his dinner."

"Now, suppose I meant myself," laughed the lady, turning the table on me with her woman's wit.

"Then I have nothing to say," was my reply, feeling very much like a fool, as any man will who allows himself to give way to his passion.

Lissa leaned back in a corner of the carriage. It was not that way she was wont to drive home with me.

"I thought you were very happy as I looked at you across the theatre," I said, holding down my resentment.

"And you?" she said.

"Oh! I was in paradise, if you'll substitute the other, less polite word. They held me wedged in like a piece of bread inside a toaster, and would not let me budge till I was thoroughly done brown."

"But you said you didn't know the lady."

"Good reason why : I had forgotten her, till she told me who she was."

"But Mrs. Ellery said you *did* know all the time that it was an old flame; and then she told me things that made me think so meanly of all men."

"Mrs. Ellery is a serpent.   I'll publish no more of her sonnets.   But you, — I saw you laughing, and — I won't say coquetting, but " —

"Say any thing, Charlie.   I was angry with you, after what she told me ; and I grew more and more careless, till I laughed and talked with that silly man, thinking you had forgotten that you left me alone.   I didn't know I could do such things : I didn't know it was in me.   I had rather stay at home: I love home best.   Our own little companies are better than those hot, bright places, where men stare into your face, and strangers, if they get the chance, say things which make you laugh, but which you hate."

"And women like Mrs. Ellery " —

"Oh! I am thankful you told me not to see her," she interrupted : "she has power to please, and she would do me harm.   I wish — I wish *you* had never known her."

By this time I had drawn my own true little wife
into my arms ; and, though indorsing much that
she said, I could not find it in my heart to believe
that Mrs. Ellery, with all her fascinations, could do
her any harm.   Such women as my Lissa are very
near the angels.

"Suppose," said I, whispering close to her ear,
"suppose you trust your husband in these as in
other matters? The ambition and vanity of that
poor woman have led her far astray, I fear ; and,
seeing you as pure and good as she once was, she
cannot rest till she throws a few seeds of distrust
and suspicion into your mind, hoping that they may
germinate, and in time make you such a one as
herself. With all her art, and she has much, she
never yet was able to veil her mental and moral
defects from me. I would guard you from such
persons, and from those who follow and flatter
her."

Lissa nestled closer.

"Just so would I keep myself so honorable in all
dealings with men and women, and with the world,
that I should never blush to feel your clear eyes
upon me, even if they should read my very soul."

"I will never feel again as I felt to-night," sne said solemnly and tearfully.

How little she knew that her words were as a two-edged sword! When we got home we were shocked with the news, —

"The baby is dead!"

Chapter Eighteen.

HE poor dead baby!

I had never felt any special affection for it. Its coming had been a source of disquiet, its leaving was to me a relief. And, in saying this, I do not think I prove myself hard-hearted.

I stood and looked at the tiny creature, Lissa leaning on my shoulder with emotions of awe and sympathy which I think the pen of an angel could never write out; for angels see no little upturned faces like that in the gardens above.

How still it was! how white, how perfect in its repose! Death is the true Carrara marble, after all. No chisel could trace such veins, or cloud the forehead with those glittering threads that a breath might disturb, or give that unparalleled polish which speak the cold king an artist whose conceptions no human hand has ever approached.

"It is so safe now," said Lissa, in her tender voice, the pendent tears shining on her long lashes.

She nestled a little closer to it, then she looked up at me.

"*Hasn't* it had a *good* time ?   Plenty of tending, pretty clothes, a nurse to carry it out, two mothers to love and work for it, — Jo and I.   Are you sorry, dear, now, that it came ?"

I understood her; and the question gave me a qualm or two.   Yet God knows I was not sorry for all she had spent, and all she had done, though I had thought more of her pleasure than any thing else ; and so I told her.

Poor Jo mourned with the true mother grief. The little one had died in comparative health, one moment smiling and cooing on her lap, the next, a direful spasm, and it was gone.   The curl on her forehead looked straight and lustreless, her eyes were red with weeping.   I think she had loved it more when she knew that Conrad had brought it there.

Tiddy was in her element.   She loved to fix up for "flumerals," as she persisted in pronouncing it. With her best red and blue turban set high on her gray locks, she made as many errands to the darkened parlor as she could consistently with her duties below stairs.   We found her once solilo-

quizing over the little body in the following
fashion : —

"Wonner what yo's doin' now, little mistis?
Reckon de lightnin' ain't nothin' to de brightness
up a dar, yender, umph, umph! Scuse my askin'
ob ye, but ye looks so mighty sweet, wid heaven's
daylight shinin' straight down on yo' little white
face! Nostle down close to de Lord when yo' sees
him, umph, umph! case de Lord's powerful fond
o' little chillen, honey. An', ef ye sees a small
brack chile a-trotting round up yer, an' her name's
Amy, dat's *mine*. I's never had none but her, an'
dat's de one. You jis gib her my lub. Tell her
de old mammy's gwine to jine de saints by'm-by,
in de glory, umph, umph!"

Then she wiped her eyes with her apron, and
dusted the casket, while we made good our retreat.

It was all-over.

The women-folks had made wreaths and crosses
of the sweetest flowers that grow, for the coffin-lid,
and placed in the baby hand a wax-like cluster of
white roses. There was no mother, alas! to kiss
it, and cry out in the passion of her anguish, "I
cannot have it so!" It was a waif, after all; but it
had gone to the warm mother heart, and to the
father who had not lived to see it.

"How can one tell?" I asked myself.   We all do.
There is a mystery in the soulless form, as awful
as it is grand.   **My** question meant, How can **one**
tell whither it has gone?   But here the faint, sweet
scent of the violets, breathed by some invisible
atmosphere, came to my senses ; **and** I said to myself, "Even as I cannot see the fragrance of these
flowers, but know it is there, so that which made
this little child immortal is somewhere, fragrant
and beautiful, though impalpable to touch."

A few friends came in ; a few friends went out,
and before them was carried the little form.   Dust
to dust !   O mothers ! how do you hear it and live ?
Ashes to ashes !   Even I felt my eyes moisten,
and my tongue grow dry over the mound of that
small wayfarer.

What do the mothers feel ?

It was very quiet after that for days.   Jo plunged
into her German ; and Lissa busied herself, I knew
not how, only occasionally on her slender forefinger I saw just the slightest stain of ink.

I took her to task for it.

"Do you suppose I have no friends **to whom I**
write letters ?" she asked.

"Not in this country," I said.

"There you are mistaken: I do have a correspondent."

"Man, or woman ?"

"I sha'n't tell you."

"Allow me to guess, then."

"You can't."

"A woman, and a very sweet one."

She looked startled.

"Her name is — Nellie Walters." ·

"Now, how did you know that?" she asked,
provoked.

"When the dean's man comes over here twice a
week, with the regularity of clock-work, I am
bound to know what he comes for. If without
much prying I see my wife's name on the back of
an envelope of the smallest possible dimensions, I
am quite satisfied that I know the writer of the
note. But hear me further: that doesn't account
for the mystery of the inked finger."

"It's all the account you will get," she answered,
laughing.

"And I didn't know Conrad was so sly."

"Conrad has nothing to do with it," she replied,
coloring.

"No, but Conrad is in every line, — Conrad's

thoughts, wishes, desires.   What could these letters be worth to her unless they came from under the roof that covers Conrad, flavored with the touch that has also been shared with Conrad? for, don't you see, you shake hands with him every morning.   That's a pretty German custom."

"I can't find my scissors," said Lissa, turning away with a pretended pout.

"Yesterday it was your thimble.   Did you find it?"

"Yes; and where in the world do you suppose?" she asked, laughing.

"In the coal-hod perhaps."

"No; in the pocket of the white vest you wore yesterday."

"Oh! and so of course I am to blame."

"Well, no : perhaps when I sat on your knee — I remember fumbling in your pockets for some change."

"So you did.   By the way, my careful little wife, you just remind me that I need that money, — two hundred and fifty, wasn't it? — I gave to you to keep for me a week ago yesterday.   I'm glad I thought of it : I've promised to pay a bill."

"I'll get it for you," she said, running out of the

room. I sat down, and began whistling content-
edly. Five, ten minutes passed. The whistle
stopped of itself: my hat fell lower and lower. I
think I must have been asleep; for I was swimming so violently when I came to myself, that I
had unconsciously broken a hole in the window-
glass, and cut my hand.

"Charlie!" called a trembling voice. I went to
the door. There, at the head of the stairs, stood
Lissa, a picture of distress.

"Well, what's the matter now?"

"I can't find it."

"Can't find what?" said I, nursing my cut hand.

"That money. I've been hunting almost an
hour: it's certainly stolen."

"But who would steal it?" I asked, as the hall-
clock confirmed the truth of her statement. I had
been due at my office for the last thirty minutes.

"I don't know. I put it in my toilet-box, and
locked it up; but it's not there, or anywhere."

I hastened up stairs. She had evidently been
looking. Every drawer in her bureau was on the
floor. She certainly must have resorted to ex-
tremes. Bags, books, vases, baskets, dresses with
the pockets dragged out, trunks, boxes, — I could
hardly find room for a standing-place. ·

"There! you see I have searched every thing that could be searched. Jo has been helping me ; and it's gone. Of course it hasn't gone without hands."

"But, my dear, whom do you suspect? Conrad has money enough ; so has Jo, and poor old Tiddy."

"But, Charlie, you forget the new girl and the French maid."

"**True, I did** forget them both. What shall we do about **it ?** "

"**I don't** know."

"Two hundred and fifty dollars don't grow on every bush ; and my expenses have been enormous lately. Are you sure you put it there?"

"Oh, so very sure! I remember the very day, the hour, the minute almost, and that I dropped your cameo ring in at the same time."

"Did the nurse ever have your keys?"

"She might have had them."

"Ah! you leave them lying about sometimes."

"Once in a *very* great while," with considerable emphasis.

"We must **go** after the girl. Where is she now?" Lissa found the card of her new place, murmuring **as** she produced it, —

" Now you think me careless ; and I do try so hard not to be careless ! "

" I don't think you are ever careless, Lissa," I made answer, " *only* when you lose things ; " and I suppose my smile was very grim, for she drew back as well as she could for the confusion. I had lost more than an hour of valuable time (oh, that wife of mine!), I had lost two hundred and fifty dollars, I had lost my credit with the gentleman who promised to meet me half an hour before, — I had lost every thing but my temper, and once or twice that threatened to fail me.

The French nurse fortunately was not called upon that day, my business cares preventing. I decided to see to the matter on the following day, and returned home thoroughly wearied out.

The first person I met was my wife. Delight and chagrin seemed equally mingled in her face, as she made her usual exclamation, —

" O Charlie ! "

" Well, what now ? "

" I've found it."

" What ! the money ? "

" Yes."

" In the name of the treasury of the United

States, where ?   I thought you looked the house through."

"So did I ; but a few minutes ago, Jo was fixing up poor baby's little crib, and there, under the mattress, she found the pocket-book."

" And pray who put it there ? "

" Why, I did."

" You did !   I thought you remembered *distinctly* putting it in the toilet-box."

"Yes, and that was true.   **But the** day of the baby's funeral, I thought the house was more open to strangers ; and so I took it out of the box, and hid it in the crib.   I hope you didn't go to see that poor girl."   .

" What was to hinder ?   But I didn't," I replied, glad enough to feel the greenbacks.   " And really you should be praised for your care of the money, after all, eh ? "

" I wish I wasn't so short memory," she said regretfully.

" Well, well, in view of your many other excellent qualities, we'll forgive the memory this time."
And we all went down to tea.

During that meal we discussed the nursery furniture.   Should we sell it ? or lend it, as Lissa suggested, to some one of the poor families she knew ?

" It's quite too handsome for that," said Jo.

" As I was the means of its introduction, I don't know but I ought to take it off your hands," said Conrad laughingly.

Tildy settled the question. She had been standing in the background, silent and absorbed, her black arms folded across her ample chest.

" What's the 'fessor want o' dem ar tings ? " she queried. " De stars and de stones is all he kin take car of. — Don't you sell em, chile," addressing Lissa. " Wha's de use o' sellin' sich things ? Dey allers comes handy."

Nevertheless, if the things were not sold, I fear some of them found their way to certain quarters known only to Jo and my wife; for I distinctly overheard the latter say, —

" Yes, I know it's pretty and costly ; but, if they *are* poor people, they have eyes to see and hearts to appreciate. It will be like a bit of perpetual sunshine in their midst."

And so somebody was made happier.

Chapter Nineteen.

SOMETIMES went up into Conrad's den to have a chat with him. The room, being situated at the top of the house, was bright with its four windows, which gave views of some pretty country over the river. These were very enjoyable after a daily diet of brick and mortar.

There is something in the aspect of far-stretching hills, undulating through all the choicest shades of woodland colors, running carelessly out in little green points of land, through the river, showing here and there the fresh reds and yellows of the outcropping earth ; the sinuous line that curls against the gray or blue of the horizon in rippling tree-tops, as far as the eye can reach ; the hush and beauty of distance, the changing sun-tides and cloud shadows, the whole combination of skies, woods, and water,— that lifts me out of my ordinary self, soothes, invigorates, and inspires me, and from which I retreat with an exultation of spirit that gives me kinship to the immortals.

Conrad himself has a wonderful talent for grouping things. There is his desk on the right, just where the window in the south throws a perfect light. ·The desk is framed in by books, and, save a few papers upon its leaf, is in spotless order. Across the room, in quite as favorable a light, stand the music-rack, flute, guitar, and musical library, a choice selection of authors of the Old World, the German and Italian masters. In still another place is his flower-stand on which are pots of the choicest blooms ; for Conrad has a special genius for cultivating house-plants, and it is seldom that we do not have exotics on our table the year round. Add to these things, his microscopical apparatus, an astronomical globe, a table or two filled with papers and periodicals, and you have a tolerable idea of the professor's surroundings.

"The faculty are anxious to publish my last two lectures on the origin of the Gulf Stream," said Conrad, as I sat feasting my eyes on the glowing landscape beyond.

"Have you convinced them of the correctness of your theory?"

"By no means," he said quickly. "The dean ridicules it to my face; and the rest pronounce it curious and ingenious, though they all cling to the old lunar theory."

"I dare say Miss Nellie's enthusiasm makes up for her father's unbelief," I said.

He looked at me with a smile that haloed all his face, — that clear, courtly, old Germanic type of face, that approaches so near the ideally classic, and in which I saw the yet finer lineaments of my Lissa. The smile said perhaps more than he meant it should. I had oftener than once met two figures gliding quietly over the college grounds, and surmised that Miss Nellie had stolen out to meet our Conrad by previous agreement. And why, as Lissa said with head well lifted, should the dean look down on our brother, gifted, successful, and able to support a wife in comfort and even affluence? What blame if, loving each other, rich in life, rich in talents, rich in youth and hope, they, being without reason kept asunder, sought occasions for meeting thus by stealth? They were pleasant grounds to walk in, and there were many other delightful promenades in the vicinity; and there were nights of clear moons and the white splendor of starlight. They violated no commands, for nothing had as yet been said between the dean and his daughter. In each heart the sweet flowers of love had opened; no withering breath had come over them yet; they were full of the dew of hope.

Just before the tea-bell rang, I strolled across to Conrad's desk.

"Aha! Lissa has been here."

"How!" cried Conrad confusedly.

"I say this is Lissa's handwriting; and this is her pen; and here is her inkstand. The proof is complete."

Conrad quietly covered the evidences with his newspaper.

"Of course Lissa comes here. Do you think I can give her up altogether? Ah! to make a man thoroughly selfish, get him married."

"Has Lissa been copying for you?"

"She does copy for me," he replied.

"But, my dear fellow, my eyes are quick: they are editorial eyes, therefore Argus eyes. What I saw was poetry: now, you do not write poetry."

"How do you know?"

I looked at him with a broad smile: he looked at me with an equally broad smile.

"Now I see," I said. "I have a new correspondent. He, she, or it very timidly ventures to send me a few poetical lines. The lines are read; I find them more than commonly good; I publish them, and wonder who the author is; she must be very young, but her thoughts are delicately matured. I say as much in the paper. Now and then, on my coming home, I find Lissa abstracted, absent-minded, serious; then I discover small stains of ink on her fingers; then, by the merest chance, I see poems upon your table. Aha! and you have been aiding and abetting my small wife!" I shook my finger at him.

"Only to the extent of helping in the translation into English, for you must know these little things were written before Lissa ever saw you."

"Is that possible?" I exclaimed, astonished. . "And she never so much as breathed to me that she could write a line."

"The child wrote them because they sang in her head, she said at the time," continued Conrad; "and I confess I was rather hard upon her. I told her she had copied this or that poet of our German land, when it was evident she had never read them; for, strange to say, it is difficult for her to read poetry. Then I told her they had best be put away, and not thought about for a long time to come, but by and by looked over, re-written, and polished. She always did as I told her; and consequently the little verses have not seen the light till now, for soon after that you came, and, I suspect, put all thought of poetry out of her mind."

"Had I better tell her I know?"

"I think not: let her surprise you in her own way; she has set her heart upon it."

"At all events, I must go and give her a kiss, for it will be a horrible self-denial to keep silence," I said, and forthwith hurried down stairs to Lissa's room. For the first time in my life I found it locked.

"Who's there?" called my wife.

"I,—plenipotentiary from the court of love, and chief arbiter of your affections,—your husband," I answered.

"Wait a minute," she called back; and, after waiting five, I was graciously permitted to open the door of my own room. I took her by both hands, and looked at her. Her floss-like hair had gathered in all manner of waves and curls around her forehead and temples; her cheeks were flushed, her breath was short.

"What guilty thing have you been doing now?" I asked.

She laughed merrily.

"I was only putting away things."

"And what do you mean by putting away things?" I asked.

"Why, to make the room look nice, of course; they were scattered about; and, if **you** please, I **won't have any questions** asked. For shame **of** you, to want to pry into secrets!"

"So there *is* a mystery! **You are** a second Calypso for secrecy and silence; but, I warn you, I will find it out."

"Of course you will, in time;" and just then **the** bell rang for tea.

I did find it out in time.

One day my **wife came in** with a great package **that** reached **to her** chin.

"**They have** just come **home**," she said, "and I had on my bonnet to go over to Miss Walters with a book I promised her."

"And in that book there is a note," said I.

"**That is** nothing I shall tell *you;* **but you don't** ask what is this? I never saw a man of so little curiosity in **all** my life; you don't even take it out of my hands."

"I hasten to apologize; and pray tell me what it is."

I unpinned the paper. Lissa's eyes glistened.

"All of my own doing: every stitch I sewed!" she cried triumphantly. "I said you should wear some shirts made by my hands; and there they are, just come from the laundry. Don't they are beautiful?" she asked in her pretty broken English.

"A set of shirts, and you made them? Why, I shall be as proud as Pharaoh if my wife keeps on enlightening me with regard to her accomplishments. But, above all, I dote on nice shirts."

"I know it; and because you are so *very* particular, I took a good shirt all in pieces, and cut out every thing, even to the smallest small bit. Oh, what work it is! I wouldn't even let Jo help me. It took me days and days, for I measured to the very breadth of a hair."

"Many thanks, my darling. You are so kind to take such pains for your careless old husband," I said. "I shall prize them more than gold."

"And I am sure they will fit, oh, beautiful! Try them on, and let me know when I come home. I am going to stay with Nellie till dinner-time. Good-morning," and with a kiss she left me.

To say I was delighted with Lissa's gift would be but a tame description of my feelings. I was touched at the thought of her painstaking, her care in hiding from me the task of love that had probably extended over weeks of toilsome sewing ; for, as I afterwards found, she had not used the sewing-machine, but put in every stitch with her own fingers. I took pains to examine the work. It was most delicately done : every thread shone under the polish of the laundry iron in minutest stitches. How proud I should be to wear them ! They would seem like shirts of mail, protecting me from every danger that might threaten my peace.

It was a leisure day. The paper was out, and nothing imperative called me to the office. I was curious to see how my present would fit, and accordingly took advantage of the opportunity. I tried my best to get into the first one : I did get into it after some little difficulty, but that was all. Something held my arms out at right angles. I think it must have been the armholes, for they caught my shoulders like a vise, and kept them stationary. In vain I tried to clutch at the collar, wriggled this way and that, panted, perspired. Oh that they would fit me, for Lissa's sake! I tried on the next. The shoulders were loose enough, but the bosom would not meet within an inch from top to bottom : there was clearly no help for that defect. The third one choked me so that I should have been black in the face in five minutes. The fourth was a combination of all the defects of the three preceding, and gave me the look of a chicken just bursting out of its shell. The other two were duplicates of the first and second.

The beautiful shirts! Lissa's gift. I laid them all aside with a gesture of despair. I was utterly disappointed and miserable, for there was no remedy ; and how could I tell that poor, exultant little soul that every shirt was a misfit? Some men might have done it. I called to mind a fact in which the husband, not meaning to be unkind, remarked, when a similar gift was made with equal love and labor, —

"They are very nice, but you ought to see *the shirts my mother makes !*"

I thought rapidly under the spur of my love for Lissa. What should I do? To wear them was out of the question ; to have them altered, equally impracticable. I took the precious bundle finally, after I had decided what should be their destination, and hid it away in a box up stairs, almost as guiltily as if I were burying something human. Lissa rarely went among the old things up stairs, so I was safe. Then I hurried down to a certain store where my shirts were usually made, and left my order for a set of shirts to be sewed by hand in the best style of needle-work, to be finished by a certain time, and left at my office. Finally I intended to smuggle them home in a way that should not attract Lissa's notice.

I took good care to avoid a *tête-à-tête* with Lissa until after tea.

"Well," she said, with a beaming face, as I sheltered myself behind the evening paper, "and how did the shirts fit?"

"You ought to have seen them," I exclaimed, with an eloquent countenance.

"I knew they would please you."

"Please me! I am enchanted."

"I was a little afraid, you know, because Jo said they ought to be shrinked."

I looked at her helplessly.

"Shrinked in the cloth, — you know what I

mean, washed or wet before made. I forgot that."

"Ah!" said I thoughtlessly, "that lets the secret out;" and then I bit my lip. I could have bitten it through.

"What secret? — lets what secret out?" she asked rapidly.

"Why, that they felt so dry and —and stiff, you know,— in fact, just as new shirts always feel."

"But they did fit well?" she queried anxiously.

"They fit like — *every thing!*" I said with unwonted enthusiasm. "Do you know," I added glibly, "I thought so much of those shirts, that I laid them away as if they had been the greatest treasure in life, for fear I should put one of them on."

"For fear?" she ejaculated with a puzzled look.

"For this reason," I went on as hastily as possible. "Those are uncommonly beautiful shirts : they ought to be; they were made by an uncommonly beautiful woman. Now, those shirts are only fit to be donned on festivals,— great occasions, you know; and not one of them is to be worn before the 28th of September, which you will please bear in mind is my birthday. What do you think of that, little woman?"

"I should like at least to see one of them on. There might be something to be done."

"Not a thing can be done, — not a thing to improve them;" and I covered a convulsive laugh with an outrageous fit of impromptu coughing, which almost strangled me, and for which I left the room to find a remedy.   But, once alone by myself, I laughed till I cried, as I thought of my image in the looking-glass, and the rueful figure I cut in the beautiful new shirts.

Chapter Twenty.

HE ruse succeeded to perfection. The new shirts were models of fineness and beauty. Lissa was radiant.

"It is the first I ever did!" she repeated again again, and called all the household to look at them. Of course I alone was in the secret; and a secret it should be, I had determined, to the end of my life. At first my conscience was as easy as the fit of the shirts. Lissa came up to me, then went back, then came up again.

"Well, dear, what is it?" I asked, not without some misgivings.

"I was thinking. Did I make *two* rows of stitching round the collar? I must have, to be sure; but still, did I? I don't remember."

Another day she examined the collar. "How can they have changed?" she murmured.

"Lissa, you are nervous over these shirts, my

dear," I said. "Please let me enjoy them, and don't worry."

I would have you know I was now to deal with the fine perceptions of a woman who wanted to be convinced, yet not against her will.

"But the collars are not rounding; and I made the collars rounding."

"They probably ironed them out," I said. "Besides, all my other shirts are just like this."

"Yes, I know: and I didn't like it; so I changed the collars just the least bit little."

"You did!" I said, aghast.

"Yes, I did. I don't see how they *could* have ironed out; but maybe they pulled them."

"Yes, maybe they did. — Lord forgive me!" I thought to myself.

I came home one day, and found her poring over the shirts, and looking wonderfully perplexed.

"At those shirts again!" I cried, thinking of Nemesis.

"They do act so strange, these shirts! they must be witch-work. I have been looking for a little mark I made. I'm sure I made it in every one of them. Jo hunted too: she told me how to make the mark."

"Haven't they washed out?" I faltered, with a cowardly smile.

"They could not wash out," she said with decision.

"Well, then, if they could not, they did not, of course," was my response.

She put them aside, with a worried air.

"I have just found out something," she said, on another occasion.

"Well, what is it, my wise woman?"

"I never made those shirts, I don't believe," she replied, with deliberation and emphasis.

"Who did, then?" I asked.

She shook her head.

"Could they have been changed at the laundry?"

Should I be tormented into making a clean breast of it? How far could I white-lie it over, and preserve my own self-respect?

It was only an hour or so after that, when that persistent wife of mine returned to the subject.

"O Charlie! what do you think?"

"Well, about what particular matter?" I asked.

"Jo and I have just found out that *I cut those shirts out by one of Conrad's, after all.*"

"No!" I said, springing to my feet.

"Yes, I did. His initials are very much like yours; and the old English R looks like an **H**, especially as it is faded. It must have got among your shirts **by mistake; and being** a little more worn than the others, I chose it to cut by."

"**As** Tiddy says, bless de good Lord, then," I ejaculated fervently. "My conscience has been dancing about pretty lively during the last forty-eight hours.

> *'Twixt* **truth** *and error there's this difference known:*
> *Error* **is** *fruitful: truth* **is only** *one.'*

I **am** a new **man** from this moment. The shirts are Conrad's."

"But, my dear Charlie, **if** they **fit you,** they can't fit him. Impossible."

"Wait, my dear wife: **you** shall a wonder see. **The** shirts **you** made **were** never worn by me. Harman's Comedy of Errors, canto nine, stanza four."

I ran up stairs, unearthed the precious bundle, and brought it back untouched. .

"I did **it** all for the love of you," I said, as, **placing it** before her astonished eyes, I also threw

the burden from my spirit, and felt free once
more. "They didn't fit, my dear. I couldn't make
them fit. I knew you had worked so hard, and I
pitied you so! Forthwith I studied how to be an
honorable deceiver; but it wouldn't do. I did my
best, however, to keep you from the knowledge of
the disappointment. There you have the truth in
a nutshell; and here you have the shirts. Take
them, give them to Conrad with my blessing: you
have my hearty consent. I know they will fit
him: they gave me several fits. Call him down.
I'll do the honors."

Lissa had heard with her head lifted, after her
own peculiar fashion.

"And you think it was better to do that? she
asked.

"No: I think it was a coward's trick," I said.

"You shall not. I say it was good and noble
and kind, and there's only one man in the world
would so have done. Never a German man would
have done that, and no one who did not love me.
O Charlie!" and you can guess where her head was
by this time, and how foolish I felt at her praise,
for I had been condemning myself heartily. Then
she raised her cheerful face from my shoulder.

"Come down stairs; I have a little feast," she said. I followed her down. In a few moments she had spread the table with a white cloth, placed upon it fruit, cake, and jellies, and, knowing my inordinate fondness for it, a Charlotte Russe.

"Now ring for the rest," she cried; "ring loud!" I followed her instructions, and presently in came Jo, Conrad, and Miss Nellie Walters. This was a pleasant surprise. There was nobody to make tea, for it was Tiddy's evening for church; so I built up a fire, and Lissa concocted the pleasant beverage. The fruit was delicious, Conrad never more brilliant, and Nellie and Lissa, wreathed in smiles, looked as if they were sharing a secret between them. Even Jo seemed to forget herself, and sang a little song with which she used to amuse me when she was a child:—

"Oh ! where has the mouse gone?
        Tibby di!
    Oh ! where has the mouse gone?
        Tibby di !
    I'll tell you what the old cat said,
    As she put her paw up to her head, —
  'The mouse has gone for cheese and bread:
        So will I.'

"Oh ! where has the cat gone ? ·
    Tibby di !
Oh ! where has the cat gone?
    Tibby di !
' The cat has gone for the mouse,' I said ;
' And the mouse has gone for cheese and bread,
And both will be right nobly fed ;
    Tibby di. ' "

I wish I could give you the melody of this silly little thing; and as to Jo's rendition of it, it was simply inimitable. The professor looked at her in astonishment, and we all roared with laughter. Then Conrad, in the spirit of mimicry, took off the faculty, all but the dean, yet in so happy a manner, that Nellie, laughing, begged him not to omit her father.

"Then," said Conrad, "I will simply say, "Mr. Raab, your position is untenable! Mr. Raab, I am sorry, but I *cannot* agree with you!'" And he brought his right forefinger into the palm of his left hand, and, slender as he was, looked the stout dean so ponderously, with his sideway, knowing glance, and his habitual frown, that Nellie declared she had never seen any thing so perfect. Presently we set Jo to cracking almonds, and Con-

rad got **close to** Nellie, and Lissa and I pretended
to talk while **we** watched **them**; and **just** then, all
in **a halo of** holy rapture, **in** came Tiddy, her
bonnet set **on a** mountain **of** turban, an immense
green veil of venerable age tied **over** that, **and**
brought down under her chin, her **great eyes**
shining.

"What yer 'bout?" **was her first** question,
reverence being a missing faculty in her cranium.
"Hard **yer way** down de street, an' was mighty
'frad folks might tink it was me."

"We were having a good time, aunty," said
Lissa.

"Pore souls, feastin' and laffin'," she **said com-**
passionately: "you ought ter been whar I's ben."

"**Where** is that?" I asked.

"Down to old Zion;" and I transcribe her language word **for word,** trusting that the reader will
not think me irreverent for writing, or her for rendering it. A more faithful, truthful, pious old soul,
or one with **a** better memory, never lived, than our
Tiddy.

"And we had a blessed minister all de way from
New York," she went on.

"Was he a white man?"

"No, bless ye' soul : he was brack, brack as I are, umph, umph! He marched up dat pulpit star, an' he opens de Bible squar in de middle. I sees him, *squar in de middle,* in de Rebelation."

"But, Tiddy," said I, "the Revelation is the last book in the Bible."

"Wha' d'ye mean by books in de Bible? De Bible's ony one book; an' don't yer spoze *he* knowed whar de Rebelation was, an' he all de way from New York?"

"All right, Tiddy," said I: "go on."

"Well, he leanded right ober onto de Bible, an' he stared way roun', an' up to de ruff, and den he said, —

"'Breddren, I reads from dis yer word ob de livin' Lord, an' dat ar word is, —

"'De red horse! De red horse! De red horse!'

"An' den de look wild enuff to frighten us. Oh, I know he was full ob de sperit! I never hard no sich preachin' afore."

"Can't you tell us the sermon?" asked Lissa.

"Yes, kin I, honey, ebery word of it."

"Won't you have some grapes first?"

"No, 'deed, mistis, not I. I's too filled wid de honey ob de Lord's counsel.

"Fust place," she continued, seating herself, "he tole us dat de debbil was once a great kark angel in hebben."

"A what?" cried Lissa.

"Why, a kark angel, don't you understan'? You white folks ought to know. An' he said de Lord went out one day into de garding ob paradise. He warn't gone but a few minutes, Miss Lissy, 'fore de kark angel, he got up an' sot hisself down in de Lord's best seat. And den he say to de odder angels, —

" 'Don't I look jes' as good yere as de Lord do?'

"Den some ob de angels, dey larfs. Some of dem say, 'Yis, da's so;' an' some, dey tarns away, an' hides dar faces, an' shakes dar heads.

"Presently de kark angel hears de Lord a comin' back; an' he jumped up and flewed off, an' looked mighty innocent, umph, umph!

"De Lord he went to his char, an' jest as he was sittin' down, he turned round, an' ses he, wid a tarrible look in his eye, —

" 'Who's done gone an' set down in dis yer seat?'

"Den de kark angel, he spoke up sassy like, an' says he, —

" ' 'Deed, Lord, ain't nobody sot down in dat yer cheer.'

" Den de Lord say, —

" ' S'pose I don' know? S'pose I can't read ebery wicked thing in yo' black heart? You want to turn me out ob here, an' fix up de place to suit youself. I'll hab nothin' more to do wid you, bad kark angel. You sha'n't stay in hebben an' c'rapt the odder chillen. I'll make a new kark angel.'

" Den de Lord, he sot all de good angels to one side, an' all de bad to de other wid de kark angel that done sot down in his cheer. An' de Lord says to de kark angel, ' Git out o' hebben wid you! Dar's a lot o' brimstone, an' dar's a lot ob fire. Go down an' jis make yo' own hell. Har's a lot ob horns an' tails, an' pitchforks : you kin sort 'em to suit yourselfs. I's got notin' more to do wid you uns. You's all debbils now.'

" Den de chief debbil, Brelsdebub dey calls him, he brungs all his angels togedder ; an' he clar war 'ginst de Lord, an' *swar* he'd git into hebben agin and conquer it.

" But de Lord, he build a brick wall all roun' hebben, *seben miles high ;* an' when de ole kark angel come along, de Lord sot in his own char, wid his best, beautifullest silver pipe, an' he didn't kar for de debbil de least mite in de world.

"Den de Lord sent out a comet-star to 'stroy 'em off de face ob de arth, an' de bad angels dey all got scart; but de ole kark angel said, —

"You's all fools. Don't ye s'poze I's got power 'nough to make de Lord tremble in his shoes ?'

"Den de debbil caught de comet-star on he long tail, an' he shook it ober de walls an' gates of hebben, an' de angels of de Lord got frightened; but de Lord, he got on top ob de wall of Zion, umph! umph!"

I have no other way of describing, but by those two words, that internal chuckle which is not a word, used by negroes when under excitement. Tiddy expressed herself by it incessantly; for answer, for doubt, for incredulity, interjection, and ejaculation.

"Den de Lord, he let down a chain, chile, thousan's o' miles long, dat a nobody couldn't hold but him; an' he caught dat raring taring kark angel, spite of his boots, an' he lower him down, an' down, and *downer*, into de eberlasting pit; an,' Miss Lissy, he ain't got out o' dem ar chains yit, an' he nebber will till de angel Gaberell blows de trompet ob de

Lord — umph, umph ! And, Miss Lissy, dat ar preacher from New York, he so full ob de sperit ob de Lord, dat he keep runnin' up an' down de pulpit stars, an' almos' got on top de Bible. Dat's *my* kind o' minister, 'cause he 'splains dem Rebelations lubbly."

" But what do you mean by the kark angel, Tiddy ? "

"Ain't you got sense nuff to know dat ? " said Tiddy, with a wise look.

" She means archangel, dear," said I.

" Yo' mus' study dem Rebelations," mused Tiddy, losing herself in her happy reflections ; while Jo helped Nellie on with her wraps, and, for the first time in her life, kissed her solemnly and tenderly on the cheek. I think she surrendered Conrad at that moment forever, and in her heart gave the fair girl her blessing.

Chapter Twenty=One.

UT me up two handkerchiefs, my dear: you know I always want two when I am going to speak."

I said this to Lissa as I was leaving home one morning in a hurry. My friends had been long importunate for an address in which I might air the peculiar views of my party, and which might tend to further my political interests.

It was something quite foreign to my inclination to deliver speeches. I had the same dislike to publicity of that sort that I have to a shower-bath. After the shock there is a glow, it is true, but the shock is terrible. The beginning is the trial to my nervous system, — just after I have said, "*Ladies and gentlemen.*" The blood flies to my head; my finger-tips grow cold; I want to swallow, and can't; I want to do several things, and can't, — one of them is, to get out of the matter altogether.

The cars whirled me to the scene of action ; an indigestible supper was in waiting for me ; a pompous president, all chin and spectacles ; a small secretary, who smiled every time he spoke, and spoke all the time ; a mild waiter, who spilled the tea on my coat ; and several committee-men, whose duties seemed to consist in flying in and out, writing on bits of white paper, and looking mysteriously at me until I looked at them, whereupon they became suddenly contemplative concerning the knees of their trousers.

I, meantime, kept up a quaking sort of dignity, and felt cold and hot by turns. My notes were in my waistcoat pocket, as I ascertained by feeling ; my two handkerchiefs rested serenely near my heart. I have, perhaps, a weakness for nice handkerchiefs, linen of the finest quality; ornamentation, if there is any, rich but not conspicuous ; size, extra large. I love the fragrance of the well-laundried *mouchoir*, the soft downfall of the folds like unsullied snowflakes, the gathered purity in my hand as I lift it to my heated brow. Lissa knows this, and, on extra occasions, picks from my cherished hoard that I keep sacred from common use, having bought them in Paris, in the year eighteen hundred and — no matter when.

Imagine my ride to the hall, my escort of able-bodied men, all vieing to be at the head ; my entrance at the side door ; the grand outlook upon a sea of heads, — bald, white, red, brown, yellow ; my solid, penetrating expression as I seated myself, anathematizing my trembling knees furiously, inside ; the preliminary ceremonies ; the reference to "our eloquent friend who is now about to address you." Imagine all this, I say ; then the wild uproar of clapping and stamping, commenced by six little Milesians on the front bench, and kept up till my introductory remarks nearly choked me for very eagerness to get out and be done with it.

I commenced — I continued. When they said, "Louder," I smote the very air with ear-piercing shouts. The gas, and the crowd, and my own eloquence, warmed me up ; my temples grew moist ; I felt uncomfortable ; I felt also for my handkerchief, and took it out in its primitive folds as it came from the good old black fingers of Tiddy.

It was near the climax of a sublime figure of speech. I had used up several ancient classics, and was nearing my grandest peroration, when I heard somebody snicker. The word is not elegant, but there is no other in all the range of the English language that so accurately describes the peculiar contortion of which the sound is born.

Quietly, gracefully, like a well-bred man, I had opened my handkerchief softly, unostentatiously, and smiled my sweetest smiles, and said my brightest say as I unfolded it.

It seemed to me that the sound I have before mentioned broadened and deepened, like a wave that spreads as it rolls. Now here, now there — What I said surely did not call for laughter : why were all eyes turned where I turned mine? Presently — Heavens and earth!

Hanging down nearly to my feet, whiter even than the "beautiful snow" at which so many editors have shivered, was —

A British nightcap!

Have you ever seen one? No? Then you are not called upon to laugh. Mine was as large as a good-sized meal-bag, gathered at one end into a voluminous tassel, which, as I had daintily manœuvred, came into sight in the slowest and most deliberate fashion, mutely appealing to the ludicrous side of the most stolid nature in the whole crowded house.

It was a relic of old London, of the Strand, of

the days of Hogarth, Johnson, and other patented celebrities, and redolent of the odors of " mine inn," the chop-house and coffee-rooms, to me ; but to my audience ! that was quite another matter.

For a moment I felt like one in the grasp of enormous pincers. A buzzing, prickling sensation, like the flight of a thousand fire-flies, thrilled along my veins ; anon I was one icicle.

" O Lissa! " I groaned, with my soul between my teeth, " what *will* you do next ? "

I believe I smiled and smiled, and felt a villain, as I gathered up, with sufficient muscular energy to have crushed an iron bar, that dreadful evidence of my dear wife's thoughtful care of her absent lord, and put it out of sight. I know I looked an imbecile: I am sure I felt a fury. Metaphors and similes and paradoxes got mixed together : every thing resolved itself into an immense English nightcap, which seemed to hang threateningly from the grand chandelier, from the ceiling, everywhere.

Some way I got through, — to this hour I know not how. I was mixed generally for a day or two afterward, and didn't find myself thoroughly and rationally for a longer period.

And all the comfort I received from that wife of

mine, when I told her, was a hysterical laugh,
and —

"Oh, I wish I *could* have seen it! It must have
been too funny for any thing."

Chapter Twenty-Two

"MADAM," said our new compositor, with his blandest smile, as Lissa entered the parlor, where Tiddy had seated a stranger, "I have, I presume, the honor of addressing Mrs. Harman."

My wife, always a little too ready to meet trouble half way, turned pale at this speech.

"I am Mrs. Harman," she said, somewhat unsteadily. "I hope you have not heard any — any bad news from"— for she saw a letter in his hand.

"I have a letter from Mr. Harman ; and, as I am new to the office, it has taken me the greater part of the day to translate it, as you must be aware."

"Oh, yes!" exclaimed my wife, her spirits rising, as she cut short his insinuating but polite bow and smooth smile. "Mr. Harman does write an execrable hand. I cannot but just make it out sometimes."

"But just! My dear madam, I think it would take five Oriental dictionaries, putting it in the mildest way, and the ghost of old Noah Webster, to translate some portions of this letter into good English. For myself, I have been in a high fever since the hour when the mail came in. I forgot my politeness, however : my name is Hodgkins, at your service."

My wife (I can see her highness) bowed as gravely as an empress, as she replied to him, —

"I am somewhat acquainted with his manuscript ; and, if you will let me have it, I will copy what you want in five minutes."

"Many thanks ; and there are the lines. I stopped the press, for I was utterly dissatisfied with my own rendering ; and it waits, I am sorry to say, as it will delay the issue."

Up stairs ran Lissa, confident and happy that she could be of some service. At the end of five minutes she had deciphered the first three words, as she thought. Conrad was at the college ; so she had no one to help her. Perplexed, but not discouraged, she wrote on, while the poor compositor walked the parlor with a splitting headache, and hurled anathemas, after the first thirty minutes, upon all scribblers, editorial and otherwise, whose hieroglyphics are unreadable to the poor typo, who has blunders enough of his own to answer for.

At the close of just fifty-one minutes, Lissa came down stairs.

"I think I have done it," she said.

"Thank you, madam;" and he snatched up his hat with almost maniacal abruptness.

"Won't you stay and take lunch with us?" asked Lissa sweetly.

"The man's wild black eyes radiated lightning," so she said to me, as he replied, —

"My dear madam, I have been lunching on printers' *pi* the whole morning. Good-by;" and Lissa added that she laughed to see him flying along the street.

It was well for my reputation that I did not go often to the country. My paper came to me through the rain, a damp and unwholesome package, smelling of ink and the bad air in which it had travelled. When I read my letter first, I was tempted to repeat some interjectional phrases not altogether consistent with my ideas of gentlemanly courtesy; the next moment I was seized with a

sense of the ludicrous, and laughed quite as heartily as if some other man had been made the victim
of misplaced type.

Any one can see, by an inspection of the fac-
simile, that my writing is not so very illegible.

To me it is plain enough. Why, then, *should* compositors and others so torture it into meaningless language? Here is the sentence as it made its appearance in "The Regulator:"—

HER COPY.

"*The skimming birds, the swift round motes of the south wind, the lively face of* autumn under wild vines hopping.

"*I picked up leaves* of myrtle, as I lurked by the sleepy *natives,* and watched the glossy ivy. Ah, then much said its *peace to me.*"

MY COPY.

"*The* shimmering leaves, *the soft* sweet notes *of the* blackbird, the lovely face of nature, *made me* mildly happy. I thought of heaven's repose as I looked at the sleeping mountains, and watched the gliding river. All *the world* seemed at *peace with me.*"

Now, if you will compare my copy with the fac-simile of the manuscript, you cannot fail to be amazed with me at my little wife's translation. However, there can be no doubt that she tried to do her best, and what more could any woman do? I mentally resolved, however, the next time I left home, to give all the work into the hands of the sub, and never lay myself out for aromantic and poetical effort.

That same day came a letter from my wife, from which I make a brief extract : —

"I did pity that poor man when he showed me your writing, for you know it has always been all chickens' legs to me until now. I did not find much trouble of it, after a while, but made a good translation of it; though Conrad laughed, and said perhaps the compositor was standing on his head when he set it up, and that accounted for some mistakes in the printed article; but I did not see them. Conrad says you are going into political life, and that will take you much from home. O Charlie, I fear for that! Our home is so happy! What can a man want but contentment in this world? You write to make people better. You find smiles when you lift your door-latch; you leave cold looks and harsh words out in the dark street. Within we have warmth and comfort, and merry laughs, and all that is beautiful. Don't go to politics, where they wrangle and hurt each other."

This was the first subject discussed on my return home.

"And you will go to Congress, and I to Washington, and leave every thing we love," she said mournfully.

I pictured the reverse of the shield, till her eyes shone again, — to see beautiful women, great men (alas! in how many cases miscalled greatness!), to behold her husband waited upon **and** honored, to **hear him speak in the halls** of the Capitol of the nation.

At that moment her glance fell upon a paragraph in a rival paper, which she had brought up stairs, Tiddy having found it upon the hall steps.

I meekly bowed my head, and wished myself in Jericho.

That small woman seemed at **once** endowed **with the** eloquence of Cicero, the wrath of Mars, and the majesty of **Juno.** Her face took on a portentous light, as she stalked back and forth; her hands struck out wildly, her eyes were burning stars. **In** vain I reiterated that it was all **paper-**talk; in vain I tried to soothe **her.**

"**They talk of you,** of *you,* my Charlie, like that? What **will you do** to them? Punish **them!** *I* would kill them, **kill** them, **if they so** did to me!"

It was hours before either Conrad or I could influence her mood sufficiently to calm her in any degree. I feared a fit of illness as the result; and, indeed, for some days her heavy eyes and dejected appearance kept us all anxious. Letters from the far country somewhat changed the aspect of her grief. Old Gretchen was dead, and the **little**

quaint house had changed hands, in tenants; for
Conrad was still its owner.

In my early youth, being of a reformatory turn,
and imagining, as very young. enthusiasts are apt
to do, that I could carry the world on my shoulders,
I had made some enemies. Among these was one
man, half fool, half knave, who took up my war
notes in Don Quixote fashion; with this difference,
that his nature was utterly foreign from that of the
kindly old fighter of windmills; and he infused
the bitterest malignity into an article which he
wrote for a paper over which he had control.

It was a dastardly, infamous production, and so
incensed some of my friends, that they besieged
the office, made the foreman stop the press, and
afterward bought up all the papers that they
could find — a few others in the mean time having
gone abroad.

Shortly after my return, a friend came to my
office.

"They are down upon you now, Charlie," he
said, "though they can say no real harm of you.
But there is one thing that may work against you.
Barnes, the leader of the opposition, has got hold
of that old publication, written. fifteen years ago,
and they are intending to use it."

"That is infamous," I said.

"Of course it is infamous, but unfortunately Barnes is a man who will stop at nothing."

"I would not have it published for the world; I will withdraw first," I said. "It would kill my wife."

"Perhaps it can be settled," was the response. "I'll try to get Barnes and two or three of the chief conspirators to come over to your house, if you will appoint some evening. It may be we can appeal to their honor, if they have any."

Chapter Twenty=Three.

 CONSENTED, though reluctantly, to this arrangement; Lissa was informed that I expected some of my gentlemen friends on a certain evening, that we wanted the back parlor to ourselves — with sundry other little items.

"Then we are not to come down at all, Jo and I," she said anxiously.

"No, my dear: we are to be a gander party, *pur et simple*," I made reply.

"And shall I get you a supper?"

I had not thought of that.

"Tiddy can wait upon you, you know," she said, a regret in her voice.

"Perhaps by that time I shall want you," I responded. Her face grew charming.

"I hope so; and I hope this election will soon be past. You are so anxious and so changed, that sometimes I am afraid" —

"Well, of what? don't hesitate," said I.

"Why — of so many things! Did you know that Mrs. Ellery is electioneering for you? She was here to-day."

"Mrs. Ellery!" I thundered: "I shall have to choke Mrs. Ellery."

"She says you have many enemies; and she asked me so many questions, even about the poor little dead baby; and, O Charlie! is it true that they write you down in the papers? is it true so many people dislike you?— you who have always made friends wherever you were, you who are so good?"

"Yes; but, my dear, political enemies may yet be friends, if you can understand that."

"I cannot: I think political enemies make many a wife sad," she said.

"And break many a wife's heart," I might have added.

"Then I will have a little feast for you, — some oysters, and some cake and coffee?"

"Just what you please," I said.

The fire blazed cheerily that evening; a grand anthracite, red to the core, sending out into the room a part of the sunshine that once it sucked

into its veins when the coal was a singing tree of
the forest; a sunshine darkened perhaps by the
imprisonment of ages, but a right royal crimson
after all.

I sat there resolute but dispirited. What a fool
I had been to let my name be used at all! Not
that I had looked upon the distinction as an empty
honor. I had not yet outgrown my enthusiasm for
reform; I meant to be a splendid broom, and sweep
right and left, nor leave a corner untouched. But
when I considered the power I had given to all
who thought they could use me, — when I knew
that Mrs. Ellery, a subtle, designing, managing
woman, who was well aware that I was no special
friend to her, had nothing in view but her own selfish designs, and that she came to try and poison
my wife's peace, — then my heart failed me.

Presently, one by one, the gentlemen dropped in,
including Mr. Barnes, a choky-looking, red-faced
man, bulging out of his waistcoat, and forever fidg-
eting with his watch-chain; and the kind friend
who had made me aware of the conspiracy.

It was some time before we got to the matter
under dispute, and when we did there was much
harsh talking. Presently the gentlemen were all
afoot, arguing at the top of their voices.

Mr. Barnes had unearthed from the recesses of an immense pocket-book, that looked more like a portfolio, the worn and yellow infamy.

"I had great trouble in finding it; I.think it is the only copy extant; but I shall use it, sir, I shall use it," he said with a flourish.

Words grew unpleasantly high. My friend hurled his anathemas at the heads of the opposition, when suddenly a soft voice was heard, —

"Gentlemen!"

There stood my wife, facing us, robed in all the splendor of her most brilliant toilet, — the folding doors and the dark background setting off her pale beauty to the utmost.

Her eyes glowed and widened as she moved forward, so like a queen.

"Lissa!" said I, taking a step forward, "this is no place for you."

She held up her hand, and upon my word the simple gesture silenced me.

"Gentlemen, of what bad action do you accuse my husband?"

They stared at her with admiring but half-frightened glances. Each began to make some effort at an apology.

"Mr. Barnes," said my friend, his voice toned low, "let me present to you Mrs. Harman. Perhaps you will kindly allow her to see the charges which you have been preferring against her husband."

"Any thing but that," I said, in an angry aside.

"Will you please let me look at it?" she asked, slowly turning towards him.

"Lissa!" I said again.

The man was under the spell of her will certainly. His hand came down slowly with the paper: it almost fell into her hands. I heard Snelling, another opponent, whisper, —

"Barnes! Barnes! that is all the copy you have."

"Husband," said Lissa, turning to me regally, "is this document true, or false?"

"False, Lissa, utterly false, from beginning to end; the product of the brains of a half madman, half knave, and written fifteen years ago."

"Then I will not read it: I believe my husband before all in the world," she said, with simple majesty, towering before them. With one look at me, swift as the light she darted towards the fire. The treacherous paper curled black before their eyes; but, though every man started forward, she was too quick for them.

I wish I could give you a picture of the grandeur of her expression; for though reason might have lain dormant just then, love made her royal.

"Lissa!" I said as soon as I could speak: perhaps she thought I reproved her, for she answered, simply and calmly,—

"I have done it!"

Like wolves disappointed of their prey, Barnes and his party gnashed their teeth.

"By Jove!" whispered my friend, "you've got a wife in ten thousand."

"No," said Lissa, quietly: "any good wife would do it."

Barnes turned upon her, his coarse face glowing with purple wrath.

"Let me tell you, madam, you are no lady."

Another moment, and he would have been in the fire; but happily I was pulled back, and the perhaps murderous blow fell on empty air. But my teeth were locked so that for a minute I could not unclinch them; when I did, I pointed to the door.

"Go," I said, "and carry with you my resignation of the honor my friends have done me by nominating me for Congress. The happiness of my wife is worth more to me than any office of

trust or profit; and while politics are what they
are, and a man must run the muck of personal
abuse, I am candidate for no position whatever.
Had you succeeded in preserving that vile document, I would have fought you to the last, desperate
odds; you should have taken back every lie, every
foul word, fabricated among your set. But now I
am a free man; my home is my castle, and holds
none but my friends. Go!"

They skulked out, one by one, like the cowards
they were, my friend volunteering to lead them
from the house.

Then, then! oh the rapture of that precious moment! the ecstasy when my true, beautiful wife
sprang to my arms, and I lavished kisses upon her
cheeks, her lips, her hair, while she sobbed upon
my breast, utterly unnerved, now that the conflict
was past.

Chapter Twenty=Four.

AND how came it all about, my glorious little wife?" I asked, as I released her, holding her at arm's length, feasting my eyes upon her. "Laces, diamonds, silks, tears! You dazzle me. Tell me, how came you to think of such a *rôle?*"

"I cannot tell," was the reply: "only something kept saying to me that I ought to be with you, that I could perhaps keep you from harm. Besides, you remember you told me I might be at the supper, the little feast. So I went up stairs, and in honor of that I dressed me as for an opera, in all my best. I had not thought of such a thing a moment before.

"After that I was restless. I kept hoping they would be done their conference, till I heard loud voices and some terrible sounds. That brought me down into the front parlor, where I stood trembling and frightened, till suddenly something inspired me; and after that came all that you saw. "I think I could have died for you as I felt then."

"Well, after this bit of high tragedy," said my friend, coming into the room, "what next?"

"The feast!" cried Lissa joyfully. "We can afford to be happy now: no more politics, no more scandal, no more trouble."

"As to the trouble, God only knows," I answered; "but as to the politics, never, as long as Heaven helps me!"

The winter that ensued was one of the pleasantest of my life. Lissa provided many merry little surprises, and a few that were not so merry.

For instance, she went out one day on a benevolent enterprise, and found herself trapped in a nest of ship-fever. Another time, going out of town to visit one of her *protégées*, she entered the wrong car on returning, and was carried twenty miles from home. Much to my terror, night and storm came on, but no wife.

What a tempest that was! How the smitten trees groaned, and the fierce winds twisted them! What voices howled and shrieked! Nine, ten, eleven! I was going frantically from one depot to the other, and then home again at eleven, nearly crazy. Jo met me with a despatch.

"Wrong train. Sha'n't be back till midnight. — Lissa."

Off I went to the depot again, jubilant. My coat was wet through : what cared I ? My umbrella turned wrong side out : no matter, · Lissa was coming. What an eternity of misery that night had been ! For two mortal hours I paced up and down that solitary depot, nobody to speak to, chilly and comfortless. At last ! a red eye in the distance, like a star at harvest time ; then a deeper, broader blaze ; the hoarse, measured breathing of iron lungs, a crimson glare, a final wheeze ; and somewhere in that long sinuous train, stretching far out into the midnight darkness, was my wife.

Dozens of people passed me. Patience : she would come in time. On either hand, some few met friends, but where was Lissa ? At last the solitary, lonely passenger, the only one left, went slowly by me. Despair seized on me. Where was Lissa ?

The grim engine began to wheeze again, — a blaze, a snort, a tremulous motion, and the train was backing out. I stood there quite benumbed.

It was the dead of night : it was stormy. I was cold and frightened.

What was that down there in the dim light, crossing the track at a bound from the other side ? . A woman ? no, yes ! My heart gave a terrific leap, and yet I dared not hope. Stumbling, running — Yes, that was my name surely ; and this trembling creature with great glittering eyes, and parted lips, and pallid cheeks, who clasped my arm like one frantic, and tried so hard to speak, but broke down in the effort, was my Lissa.

She had blundered again, and got off the wrong side of the car, where, farther on, she had been stopped by a partition, and alone and bewildered, and in the dark, she just stood there, as the cars began to move, till they left the track clear. I saw that she was in an almost fainting condition, and hurried her into a carriage.

" I hadn't a bit of money, you know, Charlie," she sobbed.

" How is that, Lissa ? You had plenty when you left."

" Yes, but I went among poor people, oh, how poor ! I couldn't see them suffer : I gave them every thing I had but my return ticket. And then

I got in the wrong car: that was not my fault ; and my book was so interesting, and the shadows came down before **I knew it ; and** I found myself twenty miles away from home, in a strange place, **without a cent."**

"Well, **that was** a pleasant situation. But how **about** the telegraph ? Did they trust you ?"

"O Charlie, don't joke ! I got out of the cars, with **that lost,** desperate kind of feeling that makes **one think one's self** deserted by all the world, that I never **had but once** in my life before. I gathered up my heart, however ; and **then"** —

"Well ?" as **a** pause ensued.

"I prayed ;" and I knew that her whisper was not unaccompanied with tears. "I was sure that help would come some way ; and the first face I saw when **I went** into the depot was — whose do you think ?"

"Well, among the multitudinous faces that cross the threshold **of** my memory, and throng the portals of" —

"Oh, hush ! **you** are laughing at me now. It was the dean.

"You needn't quiz. Of course the dean would have been there any way ; but it seemed like a beautiful answer. And you sha'n't say any thing against the dean, even if he don't like Con; for he was just as kind as he could be, like a father to me. I told him my trouble; and his pocket-book was in his hand in a moment, and he made me take a five-dollar bill."

"The old gentleman is welcome to my blessing," said I fervently.

"And we talked a long time after I had telegraphed. He was very communicative. I shall never be afraid of him any more. But he told me some strange news; at least, he didn't just tell me, but I *imagined*" —

"As usual," I interrupted.

"Well, why shouldn't I? He told me he was waiting for a gentleman who was from New York; and I'm almost sure it's an old lover of Nellie's, and that he's coming on to marry her."

"If he can."

"That's the reason the dean discourages poor Conrad. He thinks the world of this other, who is immensely rich, young, and handsome. Poor Con! H'll pack up, and go back to Germany; and I don't want him to. Though I love Germany, it isn't like America for a man like him. Oh, dear!"

By this time we had reached home. The storm had subsided. Jo had staid up in order to give us a cup of **tea** ; for at our house tea is one of the institutions. Lissa, for the first time seeing the state of my water-soaked garments, put me through a course of hot ginger, and a mustard foot-bath, and three blankets too many : and then said her prayers **in** blissful unconsciousness of my silent anathemas, while I lay roasting like a martyr.

Not long after that, Lissa contrived a pretty and agreeable surprise. There had been extraordinary flittings to and fro, stealthy meetings of Tiddy and Jo, mysteries of countenance, rapid and secret telegraphy which I intercepted, but from which I gained **no** information. Conrad and I were **in a** painful state of uncertainty, when we received tickets inviting us to an entertainment in the south room, **a** large apartment in the ell, which I was preparing **to** furnish.

" Do you know what's going on ? " Conrad asked of me.

" No more than the man in the moon ; but I dare say we shall soon find **out if we** turn our noses in the right direction, **and** follow them." We did so. On opening the door, Conrad and I stood in blank astonishment. That wife of mine had reproduced, in furnishing this apartment, the ground-floor of the little German home, even to the tiled fireplace and the embers in the ashes upon the hearth. The windows were framed in their short red curtains ; the benches, the chairs, the capacious chest, the sideboard, and the table-slab, all were there, with Gretchen's old spinning-wheel in the corner. Tiddy had also lent herself to the illusion, and sat as a sturdy representative of Gretchen, in her short-gown, woollen hose, wooden shoes, and the Dutch cap that on her gray, bunchy head, set Conrad off into convulsions of laughter. And there, too, was Lissa, dressed as I had first seen her, in half-peasant costume, her bright hair flowing in loose curls down her back, her little feet clicking in the odd but dearly-loved sabots. And another charming picture completed this pretty little wonder-play. Nellie, in a German costume, as near as could be improvised, came from some concealed nook, with a wooden tray, on which were black bread and some sort of wafer cakes to which Conrad had been accustomed in Germany. I thought Conrad would go wild in his delight over the little travesty, though there was a something

in Nellie's countenance adverse to all this jollity,
—a concealed pain, an absent expression, that
rather marred my enjoyment after I had allowed
myself to discover it.

"This is all the Germany I want," said Lissa;
"and I have been hungering and thirsting for it."

"But, you little witch, how did you get these
things?" I asked.

"Don't you know, that, after Gretchen died, I carried on all the correspondence just as I did when I
lived at home? So I arranged to buy the furniture,
which cost almost nothing, and have it sent on
here. I paid it out of my own little money; for
you know Conrad has always let me have the rent.
And, besides this, there is another reason why I
sent for it. You know you promised, that, when
we are richer, you would build a little summer-
house away among the rocks, where it could be
made just like the home I was born in, and where
my dear *Mutter* died; and we could fashion a garden, something as that was, you see, with the trellises, and the grapes and the peach-trees. Oh!
will you not some time make such a one?"

"I will, I give you my solemn word of honor,"
I said: "the other was but a conditional promise.
Next summer we'll go and find the place."

"Thank you," she said, making me her little demure German courtesy: how well I remembered
it !

"And when you saw the big boxes out in the
yard, don't you know I told you I wanted to fix
some furniture? You thought I meant to dress
up the boxes in chintz and fringe and tassels, but
this was what I intended. So when you were gone
all day to the office, and Conrad to his classes, I
had Tiddy's nephew Jack come here with another
strong man, after the floor was browned and
polished; and the furniture was put in by them.
Nellie and Jo have both helped me, — poor Jo! I'm
so sorry she has the headache to-night."

There was no drawback to the evening's pleasure, save Nellie's continued sadness. Tiddy disappeared at an early hour.

"S'pose I'd war' dese yer fixins any longer'n I
could help? No, 'fessor: ye'll never make no play-
actrer out ob me;" and off she went.

That night Conrad dared his fate: Nellie had
long known that he loved her, and now he asked
her to be his wife. Lissa and I sat by the fire;
and I plied the ponderous tongs breaking open the
glowing brands, while Lissa roasted chestnuts and

apples, and hummed and knitted ; the humming all being done out of consideration for **Conrad and Nellie,** who stood together, looking out into the cold moonlight, talking in a low voice.

At last Conrad came back to us with a colorless face.

"I am going to take Miss Walters home," he said. Lissa looked at him, speechless : she slipped off the sabots, and followed **Nellie up** the stairs.

"Nellie," she said softly, "what are you crying for? what have you done to Conrad ? Is it possible, after all, that you don't love him?" But Nellie only waved her hand, and shook her head : she would not speak. "In fact, she could **not,"** Lissa said to me afterwards ; "for when she opened her lips she just gasped."

The next day Conrad came to tell me that it was all over.

"I cannot stay here," he said with almost solemn emphasis: "I must leave the college ; I must leave the place."

"Faint heart never won fair **lady,"** I said. "Conrad, I thought **you** had more courage."

"But the dean utterly ignores me. And the man who is visiting there, a sort of distant cousin, has always been attentive to Nellie. It seems there was a tacit sort of engagement, and letters have passed ; and the dean is furious because I have come between the two, though God knows I did it innocently ; and *he* is younger than I, and richer ; and finally the dean hinted at something which I did not at all understand. It is clear that he is prejudiced, and determined to hear nothing in my favor."

"But Miss Walters, what does she say ?"

"That she will never marry without her father's free and full consent. I respect her for it ; yet still it tears my heart. I have not been very good for much " (lapsing a little into broken language), "I have neglected many matters ; it will never do, not for so long ; I must go where I can perhaps forget. But ah ! she is so inwoven into the fibres of all my feelings, all my thoughts, all my life ! God help me ! I go to pack up."

"Nonsense, man !" I said cheerily, "you won't pack up in a hurry."

"No, not in a hurry ; it may take me a month, you know : I am slow, and have much of value."

"I would advise you to take your time, my despondent friend : things may not be so bad as they seem. Depend upon it, that young lady will not let you go."

"Ah! but I told her I would."

"And what then?"

His face worked a little.

"Never mind: it is over — all — I am quite certain."

"My dear Conrad," said I, "never give up hope. There is no telling what a woman will do for the man she loves. I am lost when I consider her capability for self-sacrifice, and her resistless will, when she wants her own way. The amount of caramels and humble-pie she can eat is simply astounding. No father, unless he be a monster, can stand the manipulation of her shrewd tactics, provided she has the requisite common sense to hide the whip while she holds the reins.

"Depend upon it, that little girl with the small Greek head is planning, if she has not already planned, the order of her march and the manner of her assault. She will besiege the breastworks, and conquer the citadel, before the old dean knows that he has been surprised in ambush. I tell you, Conrad, a good woman is the finish and glory of a man's life. You needn't sigh: you'll have abundant time to sigh after you are married, though you'll smile oftener than you'll sigh, I promise you. Now, Miss Nellie, if I mistake not, is as clever as the rest of her matchless sex. If she don't bring the dean to his knees in the next twenty-four hours, I'll give you leave to go to Germany to-morrow."

"Do you really think so?" he queried, and hope once more illuminated his face.

"I'm willing to wager my watch,—the one that wife of mine came so near losing for me, by the way. So go up stairs to your flute: pour your plaints into the air, and some good spirit will waft them to the girl you adore."

"I give you my word, I do adore her," he said, placing his hand on his heart; and he withdrew comforted.

Chapter Twenty-Five.

THE dean had been away from home nearly a month. Consequently, as I delayed a day or two after Lissa returned from that stormy journey, to call upon him, I brought the borrowed five dollars back home in my pocket.

Now, however, I would go and see the dean, and discharge my indebtedness.

I walked bravely up to the old square white house, with my heart in my mouth, and faced the ancient knocker with a valor — considering my knees were trembling under me — that was little short of heroic. For myself, I could have walked up to the cannon's mouth, and calmly looked in its sooty throat; but for another, and on such an errand, I confess to cowardice.

The dean's man, spotless in attire and profoundly dignified in deportment, let me in to the dim deep recesses of the hall, on whose slippery boards I nearly came to grief, as I deposited my cane in the rack. Then I followed him into the square dark tomb of a parlor on the first floor, where the narrow bookcases stood like so many polished sarcophagi, and the white marbles, faintly discernible, looked like ghosts. I sat down on the shining horse-hair sofa, and waited for the dean.

When he came in, I knew that, metaphorically speaking, his hair had been combed, and that by no common process. Just as he was entering, he said, turning to his man, —

"Thomas, you will help the coachman take Mr. Carroll's trunks down. He is going away at four this afternoon."

"Good for little Nellie!" thought I to myself. "She will carry the day."

"Dean Walters," said I, "good-morning, sir."

"Ah! hum, yes ; Mr. Harman. Good-morning, — good-morning, sir."

"I have come to thank you for your politeness to my wife, and to pay my indebtedness. Here is the money you kindly loaned."

"Your — your wife — money !" and the dean pursed up his heavy mouth, and the lines grew deeper between **his** ponderous spectacles. " I have rather a short memory, sir."

" You lent her the money one night, when **Mrs.** Harman had been carried by mistake **in an op**posite direction from home. I am very sure of the fact. You will perhaps recollect, when I tell you that my wife is the sister of one of the professors, **Von** Raab."

" Ah! oh, yes! I discard the Von," he said rapidly, changing countenance decidedly, so decidedly that he looked almost **white**: "the Von **is** an affectation sir!"

" Dean!" said **I**, grasping at **a** perfectly perpendicular chair-back, "have you heard, do you know, any thing to the detriment of my wife's **brother?**" **And I stood** up **to** him, and looked him full **and defiantly in** his gray spectacles.

" I! — do I — *know* any thing, sir? I don't know; that is, I — I — Since you have cornered me, I suppose I must **tell** what I *suspect;* but it is very unpleasant, sir."

" I am quite ready to listen to you, dean, and also prepared to defend him. I shall not hear him abused."

" I have no disposition to abuse him, sir," said

the dean stiffly. "I confess that he has been a thorn in my side ever since he audaciously tried to engage the affections of my daughter. But to the subject proper. There have been stories going about which proved to have a foundation in truth. The professor was seen in the cars with a young babe, sir; he was known to walk the streets here like a man bewildered; finally to rid himself of his burden by leaving the unfortunate child on your doorstep. Put this with the fact that your wife, his sister, adopted the foundling, or whatever it was, and you will see that I had some reason for suspecting him."

"That is all perfectly correct, sir; but how in Heaven's name did you hear of it? Have walls ears?"

"Then you admit it?"

"Of course I admit it: Conrad himself admits it; and he also admits that the only mistake he made was in abandoning the poor little child." The dean lifted his eyebrows: he lifted himself, in fact. He took off his spectacles; but, finding that he could not see me, he put them on again.

"*You* admit it, — *he* admits it! And such a man had the boldness to ask me for my daughter, my only child!"

"Such a man! why, sir, if he had not **been**
such a man, noble, self-forgetting, altogether above
and beyond the run **of** small men with which our
humanity is cursed, he **might have** left an unfortu-
nate infant to perish, or abandoned it to the tor-
tured instincts of an insane mother. He is as far
above the ordinary animal God has been pleased to
bestow reason upon, as the planet is above the
river that reflects her beauty." And I told him
the story.

The dean sat down again, still in a maze; the
dean listened; **he took out** his handkerchief once,
but he was too stubborn to wipe his eyes, though
I saw they were wet, and his mouth worked violently.

"Now, **dean, what do you think of Prof.** Von
Raab?"

"**I am** astonished — I am *very* much astonished,
and — hum — pleased — and — hum — astonished,
as I said. before. But really, did you know how
many unpleasant comments this matter has occa-
sioned?"

"I wonder, if my wife had taken a lap-dog to pet,
to embroider for, and to nurse, if the community
would have troubled itself? Yes, dean, I have

known that much talk was generated, and some scandal ; but, to tell you the truth, I care very little about what people say, as long as my conscience is clear, and my home the best place in the world. I know my brother loves your daughter. He is a man of some means, and, as you must be aware, of fine abilities, and a nobility of character vouchsafed to but few men of his standing. You must do him justice, dean ; he is worthy of any man's, any woman's, love : so, since you have learned the truth concerning those absurd rumors, you will perhaps " —

" Give him my Nellie. Young man, you may some time know what it means to feel that your child's affections have drifted from you into the keeping of an utter stranger, and " — He cleared his throat with more than necessary vehemence.

" My dear dean, I am not so young a man, but I shall be delighted if ever I have a daughter ; and doubly pleased if for a lover and a husband she chooses a man like my brother-in-law Conrad Von Raab." There was but little more said ; but I felt that the battle was won, because — *Nellie had been beforehand with me.*

I have only one more of my wife's unequalled

accidents to chronicle.   It was on the occasion of
a small party, — just a family party, including the
dean and Nellie.   The dean, bless **him ! showed**
himself now in his true character.   Nellie was
seraphic, Conrad ecstatic, and the others all as near
some other attic as the mood allowed.

I had been talking in a rambling way about my
contributors, several of whom were named.

" And how about *Peri?* " queried Lissa daringly.
" By the way, what do you think of her verses ? "

" They are **uncommonly** good."

" **Who do you** suppose writes them ? "

" You do," said I gravely.

" I ! " she started, faltered, and looked round
timidly ; for this talk had gone on partly in an
aside.

" Yes," I said, " you ! — Ladies and gentlemen, I
am about to introduce to you a new star which
has lately risen in the firmament of letters."

I took my wife by the hand.   She drew back in
literal terror.

" Lissa," I whispered in an undertone, " who
once said she would obey me, if " —

She rose, tried to smile ; but, as I saw the tears
were coming, I released her hand, and she escaped

from the room in the midst of murmurs of applause
and wonder. We did not see her again till tea-
time.

"I made a cake," she said aside to me, "to
show that I can do some things, as well as others."

It was a magnificent cake. Joe cut it. The
dean ate a slice while it was quite warm. The
rest of us waited; and the consequence was, our
cake remained upon our plates, only tasted.

"Lissa," I whispered after tea, "what *is* there
in that cake?"

"The very best of every thing."

"No kerosene?"

"What can you mean?" She gravely tasted the
cake. Then, followed by me, she ran into the
kitchen, lifted the essence-bottle which she had
used, smelled hard, and turned as white as a sheet.

"O Charlie! will the dean die?" she cried with
a terrified face.

"Horror of blunders!" I cried, frightened for
the moment, and powerless to move.

She showed me the bottle. It was labelled, —

"Benzine."

I had thoughtlessly placed it there myself,
because it corresponded with bottles of a similar
size; little dreaming that they were essences.

"O Charlie! my unfortunate cold! I put two spoonfuls in. I was in such a hurry! How could the dean eat it?"

"Because, while it was hot, the taste was less observable, I suppose."

"Do you think I have poisoned him?"

"I'll go back and see," I replied a little doubtfully. Lissa followed me tremblingly.

"He laughs remarkably loud for a dead man," I said, as we paused at the door.

I am happy to state that no harm came of our benzine sponge-cake; also, that the course of true love ran comparatively smooth after that; also, that I built the small German cottage; also, that, as Tiddy prophesied, the cradle did come handy, and that Jo is the proudest aunt in all Christendom; while Tiddy says reflectively, her black finger upon her blacker nose, —

"Dat ar' chile wa'n't never laff on nobody's door-steps; no, *mam!*"

At present I am the happiest man in the world; though still I have occasion to say, often in joy, sometimes in sorrow, —

OH, THAT WIFE OF MINE!

POPULAR NEW BOOKS.

GO UP HIGHER; or, Religion in Common Life.
By REV. JAMES FREEMAN CLARKE.................................$1 50

CHARLOTTE VON STEIN (*The Friend of Goethe*).
A Memoir, with Portrait and Heliotype Illustrations. By GEORGE H.
CALVERT, author of "Goethe, a Memoir," "Life of Rubens," &c.
12mo. Cloth.. 1 50

ADRIFT IN THE ICE FIELDS.
A Narrative of Peril and Sporting Adventure. By CAPT. CHARLES W.
HALL, author of "The Great Bonanza," &c. Numerous Illustra-
tions. 12mo. Cloth.. 1 50

BATTLES AT HOME.
A Story of Domestic Life, for Young and Old. By MARY G. DAR-
LING. 12mo. Illustrated...................................... 1 00

IN THE WORLD.
A Story of Right and Wrong. By MARY G. DARLING. 12mo. Illustrated.. 1 00

GOLDEN HAIR.
A Story of the Pilgrims. By SIR LASCELLES WRAXHALL. 12mo.
Illustrated... 1 00

ISLES OF THE SEA; or, Young America Homeward Bound.
By WILLIAM T. ADAMS ("Oliver Optic"). 16mo. Illustrated. Com-
pleting the second series of "YOUNG AMERICA ABROAD." Six vols.
Illustrated. Per vol... 1 50

FOREST GLEN; or, The Mohawk's Friendship.
By ELIJAH KELLOGG. Being the fifth volume of the Popular "Forest
Glen Series"... 1 25

CHILD MARION ABROAD.
By W. M. F. ROUND, the author of "Achsah." A charming narrative
of the adventures in Europe of a little girl of the "Prudy" pattern.
Illustrated.. 1 25

CAST AWAY IN THE COLD.
A Story of Arctic Adventure. By ISAAC I. HAYES. 4to. Illustrated. 1 75

QUINNIBASSETT GIRLS.
By SOPHIE MAY, author of the "Doctor's Daughter," &c. (In press) 1 50

THERE SHE BLOWS! or, The Log of the Arethusa.
By an Old Whaleman (CAPT. MACY of Nantucket). 12mo. Illustrated.. 1 50

**EACH AND ALL; or, How the Seven Little Sisters prove
their Sisterhood.**
A companion to "The Seven Little Sisters who live on the Round Ball
that Floats in the Air." By JANE ANDREWS. 16mo. Illustrated.. 1 25

LEE & SHEPARD, PUBLISHERS, BOSTON.

"A GENUINE HOME STORY FOR GROWN-UP FOLKS,"

IS THE STORY OF

OUR HELEN.

By SOPHIE MAY,

Author of "The Doctor's Daughter," "Asbury Twins," "Quinnibassett Girls," &c.

12mo. Cloth. Illustrated. $1.75.

"Sophie May, the woman who (figuratively) has had the entire juvenile female population on her knee listening to her stories, with perhaps nearly as large a number of their brothers standing about with hardly less interest on their young faces, has gone upward a step, if it be upward, and now gives us a genuine home story for 'grown-up folks,'— in short, as Micawber would say — a novel. The story is well drawn, and will be accepted as satisfactory by novel-readers in general." — CAMBRIDGE CHRONICLE.

"THE STORY IS A VERY ATTRACTIVE ONE,

as free from the sensational and impossible as could be desired, and at the same time full of interest, and pervaded by the same bright, cheery sunshine that we find in the author's earlier books. She is to be congratulated on the success of her essay in a new field of literature, to which she will be warmly welcomed by those who know and admire her ' Prudy Books.' " — GRAPHIC.

"CHARMINGLY TOLD, FULL OF INCIDENT, AND PURE IN TONE."

A quotation or two will exhibit

THE AUTHOR'S KEEN SENSE OF HUMOR,

which so often crops out. "'There don't seem to be any sacredness at Sister Page's about Sunday: they don't even have baked beans for breakfast,' said Miss Bumpus." Mrs. Page, moribund in her own opinion, calls to her husband: "'Come in here, Ozem,' said she faintly, as his figure appeared in the doorway, ' for I'm dying; but don't you make tracks on my nice floor.' Ozem rubbed his dusty boots with due deliberation, ate a twisted doughnut and a half, and then stole softly and mournfully to the bedside of the dying woman." — EASTPORT SENTINEL.

"A story as delightful and captivating to adult readers as the 'Little Prudy' and 'Dotty Dimple' books are fascinating to the children." — DOVER ENQUIRER.

"Of course 'Our Helen' becomes somebody's 'My Helen,' and the love-making is very chaste and fascinating." — CHRISTIAN ERA.

LEE & SHEPARD, Publishers, Boston.

" There never was a true or noble deed in the world without some woman or girl at the bottom of it,"

IS THE MOTTO OF

ONLY GIRLS.

By VIRGINIA F. TOWNSEND,

Author of "That Queer Girl," &c., &c.

12mo. Cloth. Illustrated. $1.50.

" It is a thrilling story, written in a fascinating style, and the plot is adroitly handled."

It might be placed in any sabbath school library, so pure is it in tone ; and yet it is so free from the mawkishness and silliness that mar the class of books usually found there, that the veteran novel-reader is apt to finish it at a sitting.

THE AUTHORESS WIELDS A VIGOROUS PEN,

Which unmasks hypocrisy, and lets the sunlight of truth enter in. Her stories all have a good moral ; defending the weak, strengthening those who are striving for good, and mingling with this something which it does one good to receive.

These are a part of the "golden opinions" from all sorts of newspapers, clipped at random from

A VOLUME OF PRAISE,

That few novels of the day are blessed with. This is not a story for the young particularly ; but all ages will find it

WELL WORTH THE READING.

LEE & SHEPARD, Publishers, Boston.

NEW ILLUSTRATED BOOKS.

ABIDE WITH ME.

The favorite Sacred Song, by Rev. HENRY FRANCIS LYTE. With Full-page and Initial Illustrations, designed by Miss L. B. Humphrey, engraved by John Andrew & Son. Small 4to. Cloth, gilt . **$2 00**

NEARER, MY GOD, TO THEE.

The universal Praise Song, in Church and Home, by SARAH FLOWER ADAMS. Full-page and Initial Illustrations, designed by Miss L B. Humphrey, engraved by John Andrew & Son. Small 4to. Cloth, gilt... **2 00**

OH, WHY SHOULD THE SPIRIT OF MORTAL BE PROUD?

By WILLIAM KNOX. "President Lincoln's Favorite." With Full-page and Initial Illustrations, designed by Miss L. B. Humphrey, engraved by John Andrew & Son. Small 4to. Cloth, gilt........ **2 00**

BALLADS OF BRAVERY.

Edited by GEORGE M. BAKER. With 40 full-page illustrations. Large **4to.** Elegantly bound in Red, Black, and Gold. New style....... **3 50**

BALLADS OF HOME.

Edited by GEORGE M. BAKER. With 40 full-page illustrations. **Large** 4to. Elegantly bound in Red, Black, and Gold. New style....... **3 50**

BALLADS OF BEAUTY.

Edited by GEORGE M. BAKER. With 40 full-page illustrations. **Large** 4to. Elegantly bound in Red, Black, and Gold. New style....... **3 50**

ÆSOP'S FABLES.

A new and elegant edition with over one hundred illustrations. **Large** 4to, gilt. In Red, Black, and Gold................................ **3 50**

BABY BALLADS.

By UNO. With 40 illustrations. Small **4to**........................ **1 00**

LITTLE SONGS FOR LITTLE PEOPLE.

By MRS. MARY ANDERSON. A new edition, **with** numerous illustrations. Small 4to.. **1 00**

LITTLE SONGS.

By MRS. FOLLEN. A new and elegant edition. Small 4to........... **1 00**

LITTLE PEOPLE OF GOD,

And what the Poets have said of them. Edited by MRS. GEORGE L. AUSTIN. A choice collection of the best poems on childhood. 4to. Cloth. Illustrated.. .... **2 00**

LEE & SHEPARD, PUBLISHERS, BOSTON.